Thomas Worlidge

A Collection of Drawings

Thomas Worlidge

A Collection of Drawings

ISBN/EAN: 9783742819307

Manufactured in Europe, USA, Canada, Australia, Japa

Cover: Foto ©Andreas Hilbeck / pixelio.de

Manufactured and distributed by brebook publishing software
(www.brebook.com)

Thomas Worlidge

A Collection of Drawings

A SELECT COLLECTION OF DRAWINGS FROM CURIOUS ANTIQUE GEMS;

MOST OF THEM IN THE POSSESSION OF THE NOBILITY AND GENTRY OF THIS KINGDOM;

ETCHED AFTER THE MANNER OF REMBRANDT.

BY T. WORLIDGE, PAINTER.

LONDON:
PRINTED BY DRYDEN LEACH,
FOR M. WORLIDGE, GREAT QUEEN STREET, LINCOLN'S-INN-FIELDS;
AND M. WICKSTEED, SEAL-ENGRAVER AT BATH.
MDCCLXVIII.

PREFACE.

THE want of more frequent opportunities of seeing and admiring the beautiful remains of Antiquity hath been long a subject of regret to the lovers of the fine arts. The distribution of those valuable relicks through the several countries of Europe, and the conservation of many of them in the private cabinets of the curious, render indeed the difficulties attending the gratification of the publick taste this way almost insurmountable.

To obviate these difficulties, however, in some degree, there have been occasionally published, in France, Italy, and Holland, various drawings and engravings of valuable Antique Gems and Sculptures; but the manner in which they have generally been executed, hath been so greatly inferior to that of the original, and so derogatory from the merit of the respective artists, that they appear rather to be designed as mere sketches, calculated for gratifying the curiosity of the antiquarian, than as specimens of ancient art, intended to delight the eye and improve the taste of a modern spectator.

This at least is certain, that, if we except the collection of De Stosch, executed by Picart, with one or two other publications, there are hardly any engraven designs of Antique Gems that do not give disgust, instead of pleasure, to the eye even of the most superficial connoisseur. Those of Faber, taken from the cabinet of the Ursini, are very indifferent; and the numerous collection of Leonard

Augustin still worse; serving neither to give a just idea of the artist's design, nor the merit of his execution.

There is a more popular curiosity also, common to the scholar and the gentleman, independent of the views either of the artist or the antiquarian; the gratification of which greatly depends on the similitude of the several designs to the celebrated personages they are intended to represent, and of whom it is justly to be presumed many Antique Gems present us with a lively and striking likeness: the exquisite and masterly execution of the whole piece, leaving no room to doubt of the artist's ability to take an exact picture of his subject.

This circumstance, it is true, may seem as little momentous to some, as it appears dubious to others; it being impossible at present to make any comparison between the copy and the original: it will probably afford some pleasure, however, to the classical and philosophical observer, to compare the features and images as delineated by the painter and sculptor, with the characters and persons, as they are described by the poet and historian.

But while only such defective copies exist of these inimitable master-pieces of ancient art, little satisfaction can arise from them even to the mere antiquarian. In the mean time they can give none, either to the connoisseur or the philosopher, and must appear in general as frivolous as useless to the scholar and the gentleman.

In regard to the art itself, it is related to have flourished among the Egyptians, long before it was cultivated and brought to that perfection, which it afterwards acquired in Greece. A proof of this may be deduced from those monuments of the former nation which

are

are still extant: such are those enormous masses of stone, their obelisks, which are covered with hieroglyphicks; their statues of porphyry, black marble, granate, and other hard stones; monuments, much more ancient than the times in which the Greeks first adopted this art. Nay, the Egyptians pretend, according to Pliny, that the art of painting was known among them, upwards of five thousand years before it was conveyed into Greece. It is observable also, that the figure of a beetle, which insect was among the number of the Egyptian divinities, has been found on several Antiques. Plutarch relates, that it was the custom of that nation to engrave such figures on stones, to serve by way of amulet or charm for soldiers going to war, who used to wear them on their arms, as marks both of valour and distinction. The Egyptian method of designing, indeed, was for some time adhered to by the Greeks, who, in like manner, engraved on stones, the figures of their deities, some of them totally unknown to the former nation. At the same time the artists of the latter sometimes whimsically engraved the figures of Egyptian divinities on one side of their stones, on which they engraved those of their own heroes on the reverse.

The art of design, however, soon received amazing improvement in Greece; and meeting with all that encouragement which is necessary to the flourishing state of the polite arts, arrived at a degree of perfection unknown to former or succeeding times.

With respect to the Art of Engraving on Gems, in particular, there are indubitably divers antique agates, cornelians and onyces, that excel any thing of the kind that hath been produced by the moderns. The most famous artist we read of in this way among the Greeks, was Pyrgoteles, who alone was permitted to engrave the head of of Alexander on Gems, in the same manner as Apelles was exclusively privileged to draw his picture, and Lysippus to carve his statue.

This art was cultivated also with no little success among the Romans; Dioscorides, under the first emperors, being reported to have engraven the head of Augustus in so masterly and beautiful a manner, that the succeeding emperors preferred it to the honour of being the imperial signet.

Engraven Gems, indeed, were early applied by the Greeks to the subsequent purposes of use and ornament; to which end they were either worked hollow, or raised in relief, and worn in rings or bracelets as in modern times.

Hence, the harder and more beautiful the stone, the more valuable the gem; as it was less liable to be defaced by accident, and might be safely exhibited by frequent wear, the possessors piquing themselves no less on the publick admiration of them, than the artists themselves. The emperor Heliogabalus was indeed ridiculed by Lampridius, for wearing them on his shoes and stockings, as if, says the satirist, the works of the most celebrated engravers could be admired in seal-rings worn upon the toes.

At present, the brilliance of the naked stone hath eclipsed the beauties which ancient art bestowed on it; or rather, the latter is justly thought too great a curiosity to be exhibited, where the lustre of a simple diamond hath a much greater effect on the beholder.

With regard to the designs engraved or sculptured upon antique gems, they usually represented the figures of gods and heroes, or the

the heads of philosophers. These designs, however, notwithstanding many of them were executed with the greatest skill and accuracy, were not all originals: on the contrary, most of them were copies of the works of the most excellent statuaries. Thus the famous Sauroctonon mentioned by Pliny, and again by Martial, as having been executed by Praxiteles, was copied on an emerald. The famous statues also of Meleager, Laocoon, Venus de Medicis, and others, have been copied on various stones, and that undoubtedly by the hands of ancient artists.

Not that all such copies are to be depended on, as the work of the Ancients; and it may possibly require much greater skill, than most connoisseurs are possessed of, to make the distinction. To those, however, who do not admire those monuments of art merely for the sake of their antiquity, certain it is that a modern copy, executed with that astonishing accuracy and beauty which characterise some of the real antiques, would be as great, if not as valuable, a curiosity as any of those which are genuine.

It hath been falsely imagined by some, that such works of antiquity as bear the artist's name or device, carry with them greater authenticity than others; and this seems to have influenced the celebrated De Stosch, to select only such in his own publication. But we may learn from some passages in history, that however vain the ancients were of their performances, and however fond of setting their names * to their works, they were sometimes induced to ascribe

* A remarkable instance of this is related by Lucian of Sostrates, who having built the famous light-house in the Isle of Pharos, was refused by king Ptolemy the satisfaction of setting his name to the work. This, however, the artist effected, by cutting an inscription on a block of marble, encrusted over with a factitious stone, on which was engraven

ascribe them to other persons; so that, though the name might authenticate its antiquity, it might not serve to identify the artist. At least, such a fact is related of Phidias, who is said, in order to oblige Agoracrites his pupil, to have set his name to several of his own performances.

This circumstance, it must be confessed, is singular, and argues a very extraordinary partiality in the master for his scholar; but admitting it to be the only instance of the kind, certain it is, that there is a greater facility in merely copying an artist's name or device, than his work; nor can it be supposed, that any person who should attempt the one, should scruple to effect the other.

Nothing, therefore, but an application to the study of the manners, and an intimate acquaintance with the works of the ancients, can qualify the connoisseur to determine with any degree of certainty of these valuable remains, about many of which the best judges must still entertain a doubt.

As to the substances on which the ancients exercised this curious art, the Greeks employed first the agate, the sardonyx, and the red cornelian. In proportion as luxury increased, and the artists by success grew bolder, they made use of the amethyst, beryl, and other precious stones, not excepting even the emerald. After the invention of glass, also, by the Phœnicians, the ancients made use of factitious stones; such was the vitrum obsidianum of Pliny, called by the modern Italians the antique paste; and which the ancients manufactured of various colours.

All

engraven another pompous one, in honour of the reigning prince; the external crust decaying in a few years, and leaving the inscription in honour of the artist fair and legible.

All the polite arts falling with the ruins of the Roman empire, that of Engraving on Stones shared the common fate of the rest; lying buried in oblivion till the beginning of the fifteenth century, when it began to revive in Italy, and was prosecuted with great assiduity and success; the diamond itself not only submitting to incision, but a great improvement and variety being introduced into the several materials of crystalline and other pastes, the more susceptible of incision, as incapable of duration.

But however successful the moderns have been in improving the mechanical part of this art, they have hitherto fallen greatly short of the beauty of ancient design; as, it is presumed, may be sufficiently gathered from the following collection of drawings accurately delineated from the sculptures themselves, or impressions taken from such as could not be obtained.

It was designed to have given with this collection a particular account of the nature and workmanship of each gem; but the death of Mr. Worlidge, and the indispensable avocations of the gentleman who intended to furnish materials for such accounts, have created the necessity of annexing only a popular explanation of the several subjects: which, though not so satisfactory as could be wished to the artist and antiquary, it is hoped will give amusement and satisfaction to many of those who have honoured this work by their subscription and encouragement.

*** The reader will see the size of the gem, with the name of its subject, and also that of the collection in which it is preserved, engraved on the respective plates.

CATALOGUE

CATALOGUE

OF

DRAWINGS

FROM

ANTIQUE GEMS.

N° 1. THE DOG-STAR.

THE Dog-star, Sirius, otherwise named Lælaps, is fabled by Ovid to have been placed among the stars. He was given by Procris, daughter of Hyphilus, king of Athens, to Cephalus, her husband, in order to go hunting with; a gift that in the end proved instrumentally fatal to herself: for having, in a fit of jealousy, followed Cephalus into the woods, and hid herself in a thicket, her lurking place was discovered by this sagacious hound; when her husband, mistaking her for a wild beast, threw a javelin at her, and killed her on the spot.

N° 2. A YOUNG HERCULES.

Hercules, according to the poets, was the son of Jupiter and Alcmena, the wife of Amphytrion, a nobleman of Thebes. It seems there were many personages who bore this name; but as Hercules was pointed out by the Ancients as their great model of virtue, it is probable many of those personages were symbolical, and not historical. But, however this be, the Egyptians laid claim to the birth of the first Hercules, pretending that the rest were so called, because of their resembling him in magnanimity and virtue. It is not improbable that Antiquity gave this name to as many persons as they reckoned distinct labours, which, though effected by different men, were imputed to the most ancient Hercules.

N° 3. AN OLD HERCULES.

See N° 2.

N° 4. HERCULES BINDING CERBERUS *.

Cerberus was a dog, which, according to the poets, was door-keeper of Pluto's palace in Hell. Hesiod represents him as having fifty heads, and Horace as having an hundred. He is generally represented, however, as having three heads and three necks. Hercules is reported to have bound, and dragged him from the regions of darkness to light. See N° 2.

* Dioscoridis opus.

N° 5.

N° 5. MEDUSA'S HEAD.*

Medusa is fabled to have been a beautiful Nymph, with golden hair, who was deflowered by Neptune in the temple of Minerva: for which crime that goddess converted her hair into snakes, and all those who looked on her into stone. Perseus is said to have surprised her snakes asleep, and cut off her head.

N° 6. A LION'S HEAD.

N° 7. PLATO.

Plato was a philosopher at Athens, and held to be the most learned and eloquent of his countrymen. He was bred the scholar of Socrates, and became the chief of the Academics. He studied afterwards under Pythagoras in Italy, and travelled into Egypt, where it is thought he read the books of Moses. He was the master of Aristotle, whom he used to call a mule, for setting up a school against him. It is related of him, that a swarm of bees fixed on his mouth while he was in the cradle, as a presage of the sweetness of his elocution. He lived to a great age, and was the founder of a numerous sect.

N° 8. A BACCHANT.

One of the female votaries of Bacchus.

* Solonis opus.

N° 9. A YOUNG HERCULES.*

See N° 2.

N° 10. HERCULES STRANGLING A LION.

This design is not intended to represent Hercules's engagement with the Cleonæan lion, the first of his twelve labours: for in that he is represented killing the beast by tearing his jaws asunder, agreeable to the manner in which Silius relates this action to have been represented on the folding doors of Hercules's temple at Gades in Spain; whereas in this figure he appears to be strangling him, being all the while exposed to his fangs and claws. It is, therefore, most likely descriptive of one of his youthful exploits; probably his killing an enormous lion in a valley near his native city, Thebes, one of his earliest adventures.

N° 11. A FAUN.

The Fauns were accounted by the Ancients the gods of the fields and groves, as also the tutelar deities of the fowlers.

N° 12. PSYCHE.

A nymph, the peculiar favourite of Cupid.

* Omnino opus.

N° 13.

N° 13. NARCISSUS.

A handsome youth, who, slighting the courtship of Echo and other amorous nymphs, fell in love at last with himself, on seeing his own face in a fountain. He is represented in this design in the attitude of looking into the water poured into a bason. He is fabled to have pined away, and to have been changed into a flower of the same name.

N° 14. A BOAR.

N° 15. A MASK.

N° 16. SOPHONISBA.

A Queen of Afric, of whom the historians and poets relate many adventures, though none applicable to the present design, except it be that of her drinking poison, as represented by dramatic writers.

N° 17. LEANDER.

A youth of Abydos, on the Asiatic side of the Hellespont, opposite to Sestos, where his mistress, Hero, lived, and in his visits to whom, swimming across the sea, he at length was drowned: in consequence of which the lady threw herself off an high tower into the sea after him.

N° 18. SILENUS AND A GOAT.

Silenus was the foster-father and schoolmaster of Bacchus; a drunken, deformed, old fellow, though accounted, notwithstanding, the god of abstruse knowledge and profound mysteries. This figure, however, notwithstanding it is called Silenus, appears, by the concomitant goat's head, to be rather one of the Sileni, or Satyrs, mentioned by Ovid.

N° 19. A LION.

N° 20. MERCURY.

The god of trade; also of music, wrestling, dancing, fencing, and ceremony. He was likewise accounted the god of thieves, for his dexterity. He was also the guide to travellers, and the herald and messenger of the gods. He was farther made conductor or disposer of the dead: and, in short, had so many professions, and so much business on his hands, both above and below, that Lucian represents him as complaining that he hath no rest day nor night.

N° 21. LIVIA.

The wife of Augustus Cæsar, the second emperor of Rome.

N° 22. AMPHITRITE.

Amphitrite was the daughter of Nereus, or Oceanus, by the nymph Doris. Being very beautiful, Neptune is fabled to have been enamoured of her; but she, being desirous of continuing still a maid, fled from him, and secreted herself on mount Atlas; whither Neptune sent a dolphin to look for her: by the powers of whose persuasion she was influenced to yield up herself in marriage to the god of the sea.

N° 23. IOLE.

Iole was the daughter of Eurytus, king of Ochalia. Hercules falling in love with her, she tyrannically put him to all the servile and menial offices of the household; all which that tremendous hero very tractably performed. At length, however, he killed her father, and gave her in marriage to his son Hyllus.

N° 24. A BACCHANT.

A votarist of Bacchus.

N° 25. FAUSTINA.

A Roman lady.

Nº 26. A MASK.

A double mask, representing in profile the heads of Socrates and his wife Xantippe.

Nº 27. PLATO AND SOCRATES.

For Plato, see Nº 7.——Socrates was an Athenian philosopher, and in the judgement of the oracle at Delphos the wisest man living. He was of low birth, being the son of one Sophroniscus, a man of mean fortune, and Panarete a midwife. He has been called the fountain and prince of philosophers, having been the master of Xenophon and Plato, who have given us an account of him, for he left nothing behind him in writing. He taught his scholars gratis, and chiefly applied himself to ethics, as the most useful branch of philosophy. In his old age he was turned into ridicule by Aristophanes, and accused by Anytus, Melitus, and Lycon, his enemies, of despising the gods, and endeavouring to introduce a new religion, because he said he had a genius whom he consulted in all his affairs. He was upon this accusation condemned to death, which he suffered most heroically, by drinking a cold poison prepared for that purpose; during the operation of which he delivered precepts of virtue to the bystanders, even to the last moment.

Nº 28. A FAUN.

See Nº 11.

N° 29. MARC ANTONY.

The colleague of Octavius and Lepidus in the Roman triumvirate: he was the principal fomenter of the civil war; for, during his tribunate, he privately left the city of Rome, and retired to Cæsar in Gaul. He next invaded the province of Brutus, but was beaten by the two consuls Hirtius and Pansa. On his entering into a league with Octavius and Lepidus, after the death of Julius Cæsar, he vanquished the forces of Brutus and Cassius at Philippi in Macedonia. He divorced his wife Fulvia, in order to marry Octavia, the sister of Octavius. Her he neglected also, for the sake of Cleopatra, queen of Egypt; which Octavius resenting, made war upon him, and defeated him in a sea-fight at Actium; whence he forced him to fly to Alexandria, where, being besieged, he fell into despair, and killed himself with his own sword.

N° 30. VIRGIL*.

The most celebrated of the Roman poets. In his youth he studied in various places, particularly at Mantua, Cremona, Naples, and Rome; to which last place he was driven by the forfeiture of his lands, which were confiscated, on account of the Mantuans having taken part in the civil wars. They were restored to him, however, by means of the interest of Pollio and Mecænas, his friends at court. It is said that Pollio urged him to write his *Eclogues*, Mecænas his *Georgics*, and Augustus himself his *Æneid*. The last work he did not live long enough to correct, and therefore ordered it to be burned: but Augustus, after his death, commanded it to be corrected

* Dioscoridis opus.

rected by Varius and Tucca, who were at the same time particularly charged not to add a syllable. He was born at Mantua, on the fifteenth of October, in the consulate of Pompey and Crassus, and died at Brundusium the twenty-third of August, at the age of fifty-two.

N° 31. HERCULES AND IOLE*.

See N° 2 and 23.

N° 32. LYSIMACHUS†.

Lysimachus was the son of Agathocles, the preceptor and treasurer of Alexander the Great, whose resentment he excited on the following occasion:—Callisthenes, the philosopher, having opposed the inclination of the people to worship that prince, he was thrown into prison, where Lysimachus, being fond of knowledge, daily attended him; and at length was prevailed on, by his earnest entreaties, to bring him a cup of poison to put him out of his pain. This action so incensed Alexander, that he ordered Lysimachus to be devoured by a lion: but, being a man of invincible courage, he wrapt the skirt of his garment round his arm, and when the furious beast came roaring to destroy him, he thrust his arm down its throat, and pulled out its heart. For this heroic action he was immediately taken into favour by the king, and was, after Alexander's death, one of the captains who divided his dominions among themselves. It was the lot of Lysimachus to become king of Thrace; in the defence of which he was afterwards slain in battle by Seleucus, another of Alexander's captains, who had seized on Syria.

* Teucri opus.

† Pyrgotelis opus.

N° 33. NERO.

A Roman emperor, surnamed Claudius. He was most infamous for lust, cruelty, rapine, sacrilege, and ingratitude. He murdered his own mother, and by that means acquired the empire. He murdered also his brothers and relations; his wives Octavia and Poppæa, his preceptor Seneca, and his favourite poet Lucan. He set fire to Rome, and then charged the fact on the Christians; for which he tortured and killed them publicly on the stage in the day-time, and, ordering them to be wrapped up in coats besmeared with pitch, lighted up their bodies for torches in the night.—His soldiers, at length, revolting, chose Galba for their emperor; on the hearing of which, Nero wanted somebody to dispatch him out of the way; but none could be found to do him that favour, and he wanted courage to do it himself. He fled therefore to a cave, where he was afterwards found dead, but by what means he made his exit is not related.

N° 34. A YOUNG HERCULES*.

See N° 7.

N° 35. ARISTOPHANES.

A Grecian comic poet, born at Lindus, a town of Rhodes. He was the prince of the old comedy, as Menander was of the new; a perfect master of all the copiousness, acuteness, and graces of attic eloquence. He wrote thirty-four comedies, eleven of which only remain:

* Cavalli opus.

remain: in one of them, entitled the Clouds, he hath endeavoured to turn Socrates into ridicule, as a corrupter of youth. He was a professed enemy to that great man, and is supposed by his buffoonery to have contributed not a little to his fatal end.

N° 36. JULIUS CÆSAR*.

The first of the Roman emperors; a great orator in the senate, and commander in the field. He was also the historian of his own actions; his Commentaries containing an account of his foreign expeditions, as also of the civil wars, in which he subdued Pompey at Pharsalia, and routed the remainder of his forces in Afric and Spain. Being thought to govern too absolutely, even some of his best friends turned against him, and, with other assassins, stabbed him in the senate house.

N° 37. APOLLO AND DIOMED.

Diomed was one of the Grecian warriors at the siege of Troy. Apollo is here represented as stepping in between him and Æneas, who, being worsted in the fight, retired into the gate of Troy.

N° 38. SAPPHO.

A celebrated Greek poetess of Lesbos. She is said to have been enamoured with Phaon, and to have leaped off the Leucadian rock, in order to get rid of her passion.

* Dioscoridis opus.

N° 39.

N° 39. NEPTUNE.

The god of the sea, and father of rivers and fountains. He is described by the poets as bearing a trident for a scepter, riding in a chariot drawn by sea-horses.

N° 40. JUPITER.

The supreme deity among the heathens.

N° 41. MARC ANTONY CROWNED BY CLEOPATRA.

See N° 29.

N° 42. A BULL*.

N° 43. MEDUSA†.

See N° 5.

* Taurus Dionysiacus Hylli opus.
† Sosoclis opus.

N° 44. SABINUS.

Flavius Sabinus was the brother of Vespasian; and was slain by Vitellius.

N° 45. MINERVA.

The goddess of wisdom and the liberal arts. She is fabled to have sprung from the brain of Jupiter; and, under the name of Pallas, presideth over arms and the events of war.

N° 46. JULIUS CÆSAR.

See N° 36.

N° 47. HERCULES.

See N° 7.

N° 48. SEMIRAMIS.

The wife of Ninus, king of Assyria. After the death of her husband, she put on man's apparel, and personated her own son: in which disguise, having done many wonderful exploits, she discovered herself, and was held in admiration by her people. She conquered

conquered Æthiopia, and penetrated into India; but, entertaining an incestuous passion for her own son, she was slain by him after reigning forty-two years.

N° 49. SCIPIO.

There were several men of rank and eminence of this name in Rome: particularly Africanus Major, who conquered Hannibal; and Scipio Æmilianus or Africanus Minor, who subdued Numantia, and destroyed Carthage. There was also a Scipio Nasica, a very popular man, and adjudged by the Roman senate to be the best man in Rome. This is probably the head of the latter.

N° 50. APOLLO.

The god of physic, music, divination, and poetry. In heaven he is called Sol, on earth Bacchus, and below Apollo. He is also called Phœbus.

N° 51. GANYMEDE.

The son of Tros, king of Troy. The poets fable that Jupiter, in the form of an eagle, carried him up to heaven, and made him his cup-bearer. This fable is evidently pointed at by the figure.

N° 52. THE ZODIAC AND QUADRIGA.

The twelve signs of the zodiac round the constellation of quadriga. The quadriga was frequently put on the reverse of medals, struck by the Romans on occasion of their victories. Here it is the goddess Victory herself, who hovers over the car. Sometimes the conqueror was placed in it.

N° 53. ÆSCULAPIUS.

The son of Apollo, fabled to be so skilful in physic, that he raised people from the dead: on which account Pluto is said to have complained of him to Jupiter, who thereupon struck him with a thunderbolt.

N° 54. SOCRATES*.

See N° 27.

N° 55. ANTINOUS.

A favourite of the emperor Hadrian, whom the Greeks, in order to please that prince, consecrated, and struck medals in his honour.

* Agathemeri opus.

N° 56.

N° 56. SAPPHO.

See N° 58.

N° 57. MERCURY.

The god of music, wrestling, dancing, fencing, good breeding, trading, thieving, and many other arts. Indeed he is said to have so much business on his hands above and below, that he is without rest day or night. His more particular office, however, is that of herald or messenger to the gods.

N° 58. CICERO.

Marcus Tullius Cicero was the most celebrated of all the Roman orators. His talents raising him early to the office of consul, he was the first who was honoured with the title of Father of his country: he was a zealous defender of the public liberty, and the best advocate for private property.—During the time of Catiline's conspiracy, he was banished the city by Claudius the Tribune: he was soon after honourably restored. In the civil wars he sided with Pompey, and was put to death by order of Marc Antony, in the sixty-third year of his age.

N° 59. AN INFANT HERCULES.

Hercules is here represented as strangling two serpents which attacked him when he was in his cradle.

N° 60. MINERVA.

See N° 45.

N° 61. A MASK OF SILENUS.

See N° 18.

N° 62. A LION.

N° 63. JULIA.

There were several Roman empresses and ladies of rank so called; the most remarkable were the daughter and grand-daughter of Augustus, both women of ill, dissolute character.

N° 64. NEPTUNE.

See N° 39.

Nº 65. MESSALINA.

The daughter of Messala and wife of Claudius Cæsar; a most abandoned prostitute, put to death, by order of her husband, for marrying Silius her gallant.

Nº 66. A PHILOSOPHER.

Nº 67. MEDUSA.

See Nº 5.

Nº 68. CUPID AND A BOAR.

See Nº 178.

Nº 69. HERCULES.

See Nº 2.

Nº 70. A SOW.

N° 71. DEA DELLA SALUTE.

The goddess of health.

N° 72. APOLLO.

See N° 50.

N° 73. CAIUS MARIUS.

A Roman of mean birth and extraction, but raised by his valour to the highest offices of the state. He overcame Jugertha in Numidia, the Cimbri in Gaul, and the Germans in Italy; but quarrelling afterwards with Sylla, who took part with the nobles against the plebeians, the greatest outrages were committed by both parties. Being at length overcome, however, Caius was compelled to skulk in the marshes of Minturnæ, where he was at length discovered and imprisoned. In this situation a common soldier was sent to kill him; but the fellow was so terrified by his stern looks and speech, that he durst not attempt it: so that he escaped from prison and went into Africa, where he lived in banishment till recalled by Cinna; when he was made consul the seventh time, and died in his consulship at the age of sixty-eight years.

N° 74. MEDUSA.

See N° 5.

N° 75. CLEOPATRA

A queen of Egypt, sister and wife to the last Ptolemy. She had an amour with Julius Cæsar, and afterwards with Marc Antony, who divorced his wife Octavia, sister to Augustus, on her account. This so irritated Augustus, that he declared war against him, and overcame him in a sea-fight at Actium. On this, Antony despairing, killed himself, and Cleopatra fled to Alexandria; whither being pursued, and finding there was no hope of meeting with any favour at the hands of Augustus, she put two asps to her breasts, and expired on the tomb of Antony.

N° 76. HERCULES BIBAX*.

Hercules drinking. See N° 5.

N° 77. SILENUS.

See N° 18.

N° 78. DIOMED.

See N° 57.

N° 79. AN URN.

* Adeonnis opus.

N° 80. JUPITER.

See N° 40.

N° 81. A HORSE.

N° 82. LEPIDUS.

There were several Romans of this name.—The most celebrated is he who joined with Marc Antony and Octavius Cæsar, to constitute that administration of government which was thence called the triumvirate.

N° 83. A BACCHANAL.

See N° 24.

N° 84. AGRIPPINA.

The daughter of Germanicus, mother of Nero, and sister to Caligula, first married to Domitius, and afterwards to Claudius, whom she poisoned, that she might make her son Nero emperor.

N° 85. PHILIP OF MACEDON*.

The king of Macedon, and father to Alexander the Great.

N° 86. MERCURY.

See N° 20.

N° 87. ALEXANDER†.

Surnamed the Great; a prince of most extraordinary spirit; educated under Callisthenes and Aristotle: fond of learning and learned men, but more of military glory. He began his enterprises in the twentieth year of his age, and in about twelve years conquered Greece, Persia, and almost all the East, comprehending the greatest part of the then known world.

N° 88. TIBERIUS.

The third emperor of Rome. A dissolute and cruel tyrant.

N° 89. MARCUS BRUTUS.

An acute Roman orator, and good civilian; an intimate friend to Cicero, and anthor of three books on jurisprudence.

* Pyrgotelis opus.
† Pyrgotelis opus.

N° 90. PTOLEMY.

The general name of the Egyptian kings, after the time of Alexander the Great. The most considerable among them was Ptolemy Philadelphus, a man of great learning, who furnished the great library at Alexandria with seven hundred thousand volumes, and, at the instance of Demetrius, caused the Old Testament to be translated into Greek.

N° 91. JUPITER AMMON.

Jupiter was worshipped at his temple in the deserts of Libya under the form of a ram; the horns of which animal are affixed to the head in the figure.

N° 92. VACCA.

A Cow.

N° 93. PTOLEMY.

See N° 90.

N° 94. LUCILLA.

N° 95. CARACALLA.

M. Aurelius Antoninus, who was so called on account of a Gaulish garment he used to wear in war. He was declared Cæsar, and made partner in the empire with Geta, his brother by the father's side, whom he afterwards killed that he might have no competitor to the throne. He beheaded also the great lawyer Papinian, because he refused to excuse or justify the murder of his brother. He was a dissolute prince, much addicted to wine and women, and was killed by one of his own centurions in the forty-third year of his age.

N° 96. IOLE.

See N° 23.

N° 97. PLUTO.

The king of Hell, according to the poets.

N° 98. HANNIBAL.

A politic and valiant general of Carthage, who carried on a war against the Romans for sixteen years together; during which time he won many battles: but, being at last defeated, and reduced to great extremities, he took a dose of poison, which it is said he kept in a ring for that purpose.

N° 99. METRODORUS.

An Athenian philosopher, scholar to Carneades, or perhaps Metrodorus Melicus, inventor of an art of memory.

N° 100. SAPPHO.

See N° 38.

N° 101. BACCHUS.

The inventor, and therefore called the God of Wine.

N° 102. JUPITER.

See N° 91.

N° 103. A FAUN'S HEAD.

See N° 11.

N° 104. JULIA PIA.

See N° 63.

N° 105. SCIPIO AFRICANUS.

Africanus Major. See N° 49.

N° 106. A PHILOSOPHER.

Supposed to be Carneades.

N° 107. SABINA.

The daughter of Poppæus Sabinus, a noble Roman of consular dignity.

N° 108. A SATYR.

A fictitious being, whose upper part resembles a man, except that it has horns on its head. Its lower part resembles the form of a goat. The satyrs are feigned to be inhabitants of the woods, and are the constant attendants on Bacchus and the nymphs.

N° 109. HOMER.

An ancient Greek poet, so famous that seven of the greatest cities of Greece contended for the honour of being his birth-place, which is most generally ascribed to Smyrna. The poets called him frequently Mæonides, as being the son of Mæon. His Iliad and Odyssey have been translated into all the modern languages, and are universally known.

N° 110. A BACCHANAL.

See N° 24.

N° 111. HERCULES.

See N° 2.

N° 112. EPICURUS.

A philosopher of Athens; the scholar of Xenocrates and Aristotle. A man very different from his followers, who, by mistaking his doctrines, fell into those excesses which disgraced his sect; he himself being remarkably temperate, and placing his summum bonum in the tranquillity of the mind.

N° 113. VITELLIUS.

The ninth Roman emperor, a miser and glutton. His army deserting him in favour of Vespasian, he was put to death in the most ignominious manner, in the fifty-seventh year of his age; both his brother and son perishing with him.

N° 114. A MASK.

N° 115. DIOMED AND ULYSSES*.

Diomed was king of Ætolia, and one of the Grecian worthies in the Trojan war. Ulysses was king of the islands of Ithaca and Dulichium. He was esteemed the most eloquent and politic commander of all the Greeks who went to the siege of Troy: to which, however, he was so much averse, that he feigned madness to be excused from going; presaging the hardships he should undergo.

N° 116. A FAUN.

See N° 11.

N° 117. A CHIMERA.

N° 118. JUPITER AMMON.

See N° 91.

N° 119. JUPITER AND ISIS.

Isis, or Io, a goddess, who is said to have changed Iphis, the daughter of Telethusa, into a man, that she might prove a husband to Ianthe.

* Felicis Calpurnii Severi opus.

N° 120. CENTAURS.

The Centaurs were a people of Thessaly, near mount Pelion, who first broke horses for war: hence, being seen on horseback at a distance, they were supposed to be creatures that had the upper part of their bodies like the human species, and the lower part like that of a horse.

N° 121. AGRIPPA.

The son-in-law of Augustus Cæsar; the first of the Romans that was honoured with a naval garland, which he received of that emperor for his naval victory over Sextus Pompeius. There are several medals of this Agrippa to be met with in the cabinets of the curious.

N° 122. OMPHALE.

A queen of Lydia, with whom Hercules being in love, he became her slave; changing with her his club and lion's skin for a spindle and distaff, and suffering pictures and statues of himself in that situation.

N° 123. A LION.

N° 124. JUPITER SERAPHI.

See N° 40.

N° 125. MERCURY.

See N° 20.

N° 126. IOLE.

See N° 25.

N° 127. GERMANICUS.

The son of Nero Drusus, a youth of great courage and courtesy; being universally beloved, and therefore designed by Augustus for his successor. He was adopted by Tiberius; but was suspected to be poisoned at about thirty years of age.

N° 128. HERCULES.

See N° 2.

N° 129. HORACE.

The prince of Roman lyric poetry, born at Venusium, a town of Apulia, in mean circumstances. He went thence to Rome, where he first learned to read, but afterwards studied philosophy at Athens; attaching himself, however, to no particular sect. Getting acquainted

acquainted with Mecænas, he was recommended to Augustus Cæsar, with whom he was in great favour.

N° 130. ANTIOCHUS.

A king of Syria, surnamed the Hawk; and also called Antiochus the Great.

N° 131. POMPEY.

A valiant commander of the Romans, who gained many victories; but was at last overcome by Cæsar, and slain in his flight in Egypt. There were several other Romans of rank so called; but this was distinguished by the title of Pompey the Great.

N° 132. VICTORY.

Victoria, the goddess of Victory; in whose honour the Romans struck abundance of medals.

N° 133. A GIRL.

N° 134. AUGUSTUS AND LIVIA*.

The second emperor of Rome, nephew to Julius Cæsar by his sister. A prince so beloved by the Romans, that all the succeeding emperors, for the sake of good luck, assumed his name. See N° 91.

* Dioscoridis opus.

N° 135. SILENUS.

The foster-father of Bacchus. He is usually represented as a little, flat-nosed, bald, fat, tun-bellied, drunken, old fellow, riding on an ass. Notwithstanding his external deformity, however, he is accounted the god of abstruse mysteries and profound science. See N° 18.

N° 136. THE APOTHEOSIS OF FAUSTINA.

The deification of Faustina; a custom begun among the Romans in the time of Augustus.

N° 137. POPEA.

A Roman lady, the wife of Rufius Crispus, but introduced to Nero by the recommendation of Otho.

N° 138. PTOLEMY.

See N° 90.

N° 139. HELIOGABULUS AND JULIA PAULE.

Heliogabulus was a Roman emperor, remarkable for his high and luxurious living. Julia Paule, a Roman lady, his mistress.

N° 140. A WOMAN'S HEAD.

N° 141. HERCULES WITH A BULL*.

This figure is supposed by some rather to represent Milo, who at the Olympic games would carry an ox a furlong without breathing.

N° 142. JUPITER AND LEDA.

Leda was the daughter of Thestius, and wife of Tyndarus, king of Laconia. The poets feign that Jupiter embraced her during her pregnancy, in the shape of a swan: in consequence of which she laid two eggs, the one yielding Pollux and Helena, the other Castor and Clytemnestra.

N° 143. SALVATOR MUNDI.

N° 144. THE TRAGIC MUSE.

N° 145. DISCOBULUS.

A famous quoit player at the Olympic games.

N° 146. APOLLO.

See N° 50.

N° 147. ANTINOUS.

See N° 55.

* Anterolis opus.

N° 148.

N° 148. CICERO.

See N° 58.

N° 149. SAPPHO.

See N° 58.

N° 150. HERCULES REPOSING.

See N° 8.

N° 151. ACHILLES*.

The son of Peleus, king of Thessaly, and, as the poets say, Thetis the goddess of the sea. His mother is fabled to have dipped him in the Styx when a child, to render him invulnerable; but neglected bathing that part of the foot by which she held him. He was tutored by Chiron, the Centaur, to learn to ride the great horse, and play on the lyre, agreeable to the attitude in which he is here represented.——His mother was told by the oracle, that if he went to the wars of Troy, with the other Grecian princes, he should be slain there. In consequence of which she disguised him in women's apparel, and concealed him among the daughters of Lycomedes; one of whom, Deidamia, the mother of Pyrrhus, he got with child. But it being prophesied, that unless Achilles joined the besiegers Troy could not be reduced, the crafty Ulysses discovered him. His armour, at the request of Thetis, was made by Vulcan, and so tempered,

* Pamphili opus.

pered, that it could not be penetrated by human force; a needless incumbrance after his mother's precaution, as he only wanted armour for his heel.

N° 152 and 153. TWO HEADS.

N° 154. CERES.

The goddess of corn and tillage.

N° 155. APOLLO.

See N° 30.

N° 156. A BULL DRINKING.

N° 157. LAOCOON.

The priest of Apollo at Troy, who pierced the Trojan horse with his spear, and made the arms within to clash: at which violence offered to Pallas, she sent two serpents out of the sea, who destroyed him and his two sons.

N° 158. SABINA.

N° 159. A PHILOSOPHER.

N° 160. SILENUS.

See N° 135.

N° 161. JUPITER TONANS.

See N° 40.

N° 162. ALEXANDER SEVERUS.

The twenty-first emperor of Rome, who, by his virtue and prudence, restored the Roman state, which had been so disordered by his predecessor Heliogabalus. He took the name of Alexander from his being born at Arcæna, in a temple dedicated to Alexander the Great.

N° 163. DOMITIAN.

The twelfth emperor of Rome, son to Vespasian, and brother to Titus: a prince of a cruel disposition, and a great persecutor of the Christians. It is said he amused himself in private with killing flies, by running them through with a needle; a circumstance that occasioned Crispus, when asked who was with the emperor, to reply, "Not so much as a fly."

N° 164. MINERVA.

See N° 45.

N° 165. A SOW.

N° 166. ÆSCULAPIUS.

The god of physic. See N° 33.

Nº 167. A FEMALE FIGURE.

Nº 168. A CHIMERA.

Nº 169. BACCHUS.

See Nº 110.

Nº 170. A TYGER.

Nº 171. ENDYMION.

A shepherd, the son of Athlus, with whom, because he found out the course of the moon, the poets feign Cynthia to have fallen desperately in love. To obtain a kiss of him, they say, she threw him into a profound sleep on mount Latmus, agreeable to the figure.

Nº 172. PERSEUS.

The son of Jupiter and Danae; to whom, when he grew up, Mercury gave a faulchion, Jupiter a pair of wings for his feet, and Minerva a shield. Thus accoutred he attacked Medusa, when her snakes were asleep, and cut off her head, which he is represented here as holding in his hand.

Nº 173. A WASP.

N° 174. HERCULES.

See N° 2.

N° 175. A COCK.

N° 176. CUPID.

The god of love. He is here represented as having laid his bow and arrows aside, and in pursuit of a butterfly.

N° 177. APOLLO.

See N° 50.

N° 178. OMPHALE.

See N° 122.

N° 179. ULYSSES.

See N° 115.

N° 180. CYRUS.

An eastern emperor, the founder of the Persian monarchy. He was the son of Cambyses by Mandane, the daughter of Astyages. It was foretold at his birth, that he should rule over Asia, and drive Astyages from his kingdom; which the latter took many ineffectual means

means to prevent. He first united the Medes and Persians, subdued the Assyrians, took Babylon, overthrew the Lydians, and took their king Crœsus prisoner. After this he set the Jews at liberty who had been detained in captivity at Babylon, and sent them to their own country, with leave to rebuild the temple of Jerusalem. He was a prince greatly admired for his personal qualifications, but particularly for his extensive memory. Being engaged, however, in a war with the Scythians, he was slain, with two thousand of his men, in an ambush laid for them by queen Tomyris, who, in revenge for the death of her son, caused the head of Cyrus to be cut off, and thrown into a vessel full of blood, saying, "There, now drink your fill of what you have so long thirsted after."

F I N I S.

Printed by Bensley and Son,
Bolt Court, Fleet Street, London.

Young Hercules on [illegible] Montague
according to Act of Parliament [illegible]

Hercules [illegible]

Lyons Head on [illegible]

according to Act of Parliament [illegible]

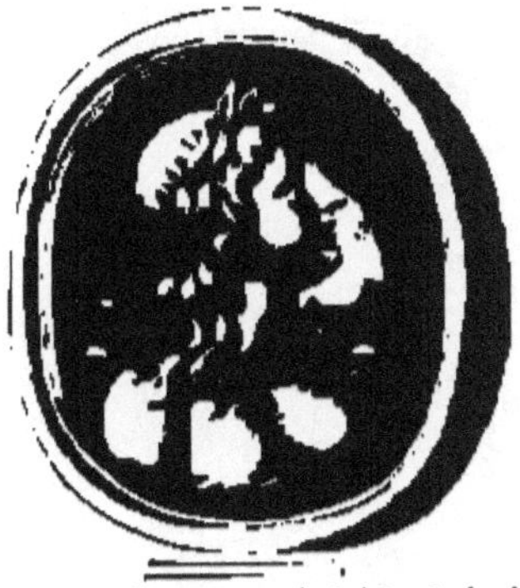

[illegible]
[illegible] of Parliament [illegible]

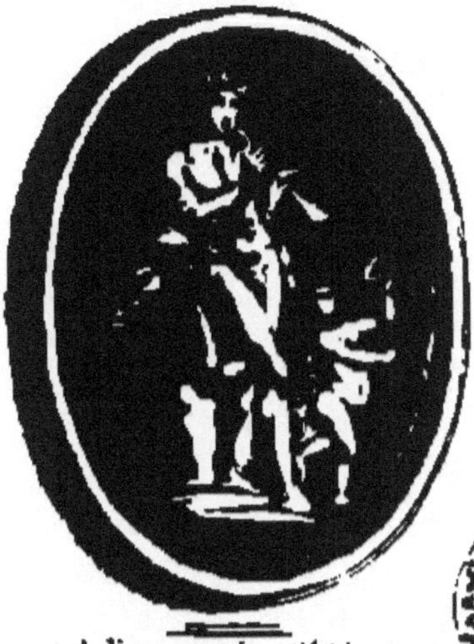

A Faun [illegible]

[illegible] Parliament [illegible]

Psyche on Altar L.d Montague

[illegible]

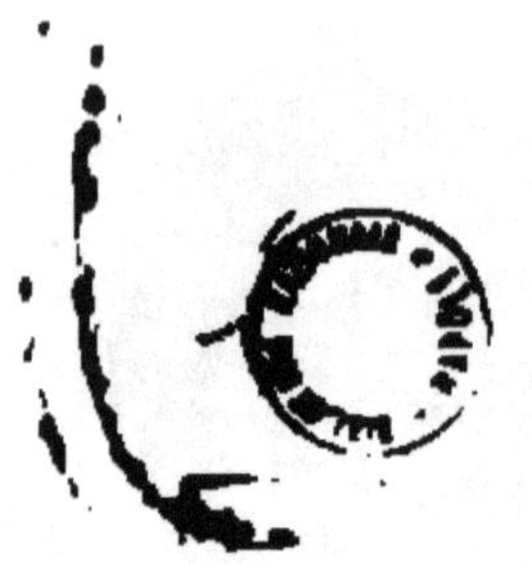

Narcissus

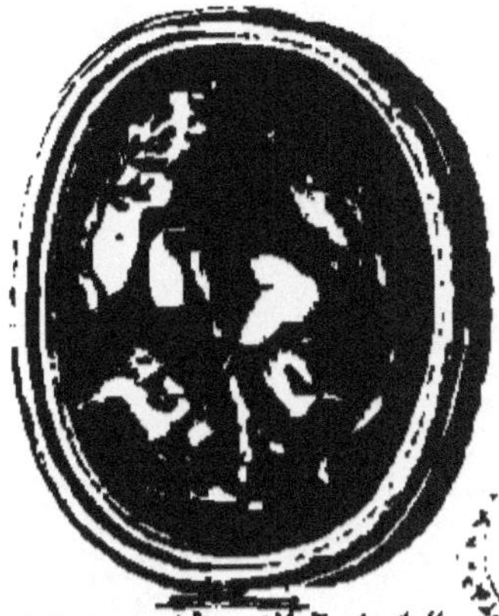

1 A Boar on [illegible]

[illegible]

A Mask on Cin. Jn. Montague

According to Act of Parliament by Montague

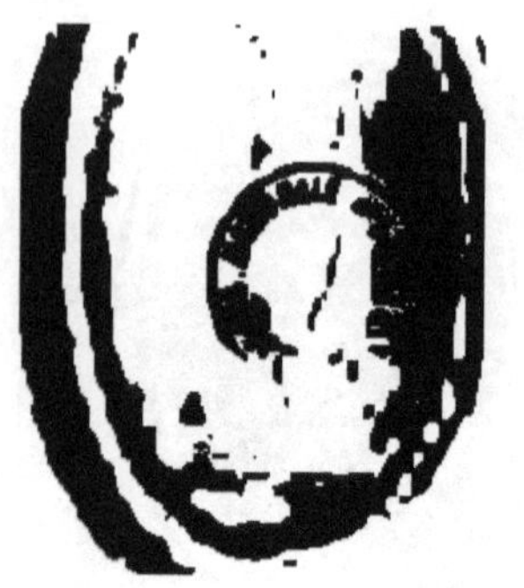

Leander, on a [illegible]

according to Act of Parliament [illegible]

Silenus and a Goat

on a Beryl. [illegible]

[illegible]

A Lion, on Beryl, [illegible]

[illegible]

Mercury, on Hiacynth L.d Chesterfield

according to Act of Parliament

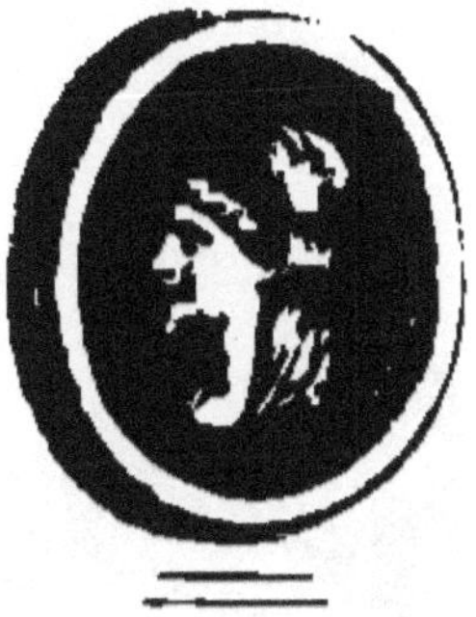

Iavia [illegible]

[illegible]

Amphitrite on Cor. Ld Clanbrassill.

According to Act of Parliament T. Worlidge sculp

[illegible] Montague.

According to Act of Parliament [illegible]

A Bacchanti, on Cornel. Ld Montague —

according to Act of Parliament

[illegible]

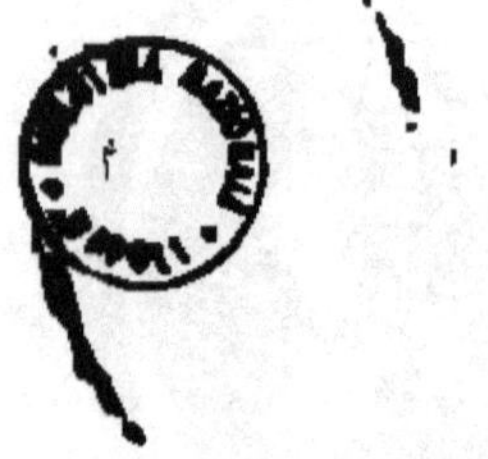

[illegible] on [illegible] L.d Montague,

answering to that of [illegible]

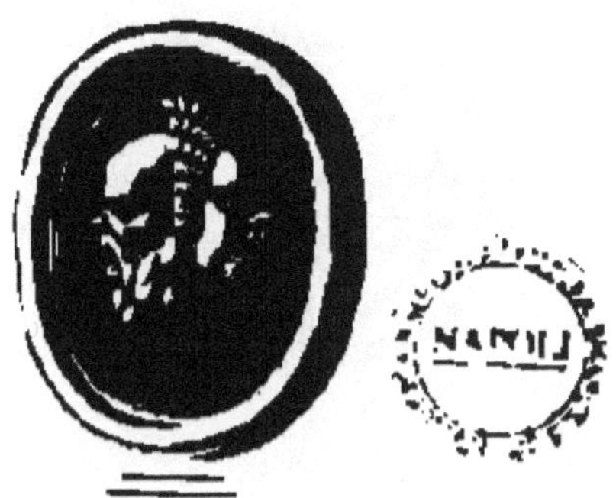

[illegible]

[illegible]

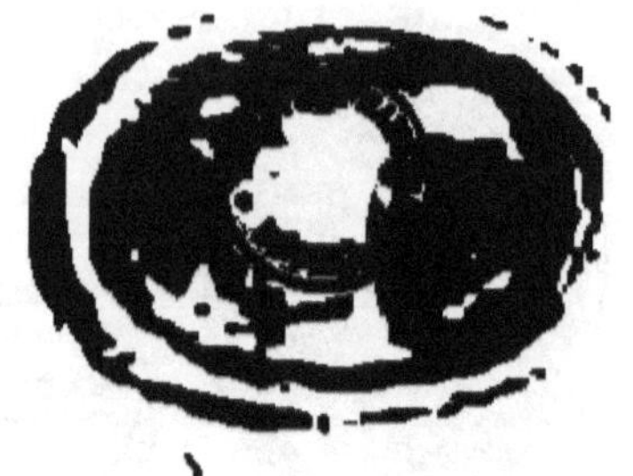

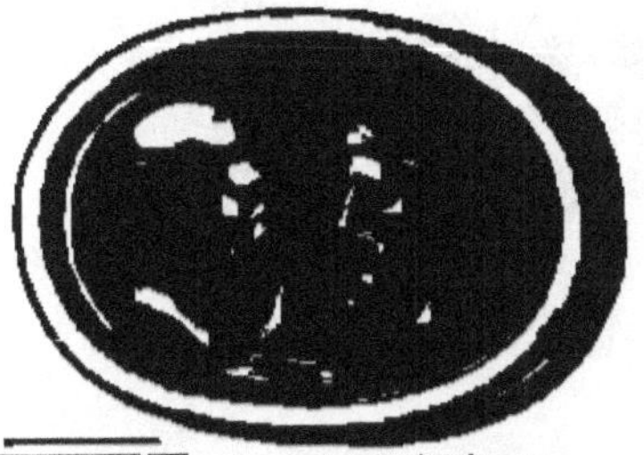

Plate 1 Socrates on [illegible] Bessborough

[illegible]

A Venus on [illegible] Ly. Montague

according to Act of Parliament [illegible] Worlidge [illegible]

Marc Anthony [illegible]

[illegible]

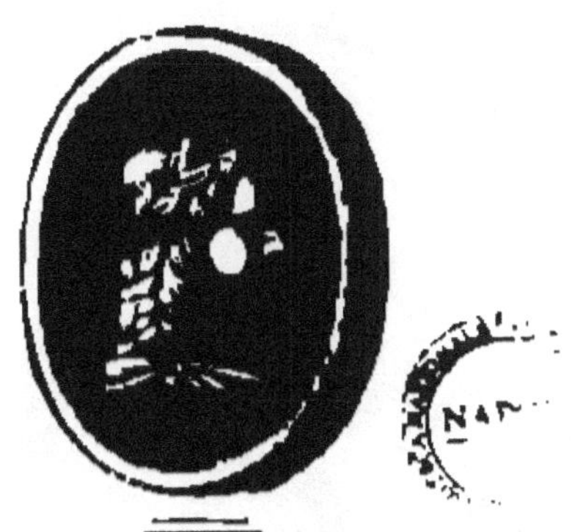

Virgil on Cor. L^{d}. Montague.

according to Act of Parliament [illegible]

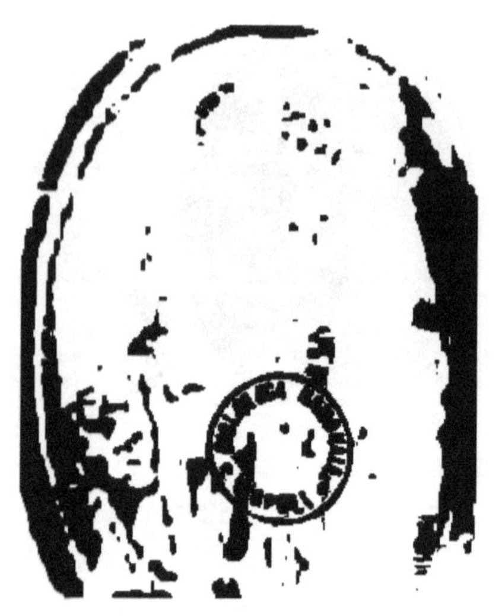

Hercules & Iole on Am. Florentine.

According to Act of Parliament [illegible]

Bacchus on Ch. M.rs Montague
London as Act of Parliament [illegible]

Nero on Corn. Florentine.

According to Act of Parliament [illegible]

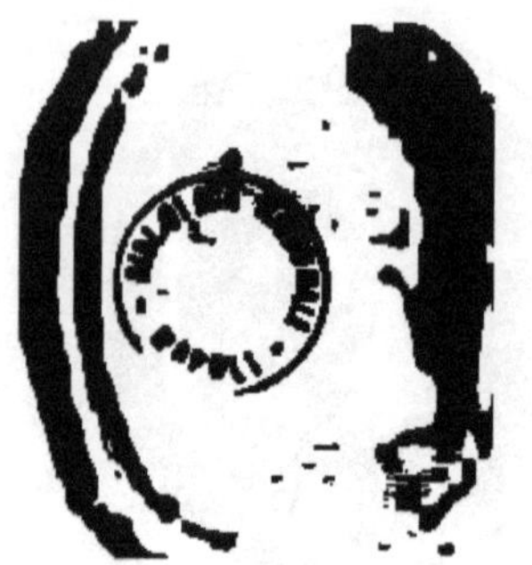

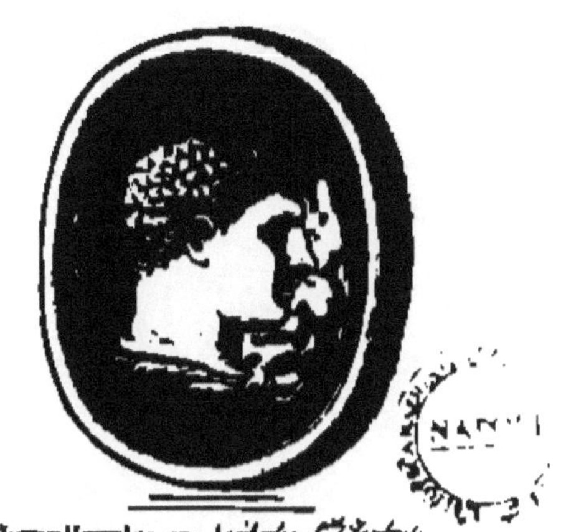

Young Hercules on a [illegible]
[illegible] of Parliament [illegible]

Aristophanes on Cor.. S King of y. Naples..

[illegible] to that of Parliament [illegible]

Jul. Caesar on [illegible] Mat.w Duane Esq.r

[illegible] to Act of Parliament [illegible]

Apollo & Diomed on Ber Lᵈ Besborough

According to Act of Parliament T. Worlidge sc.

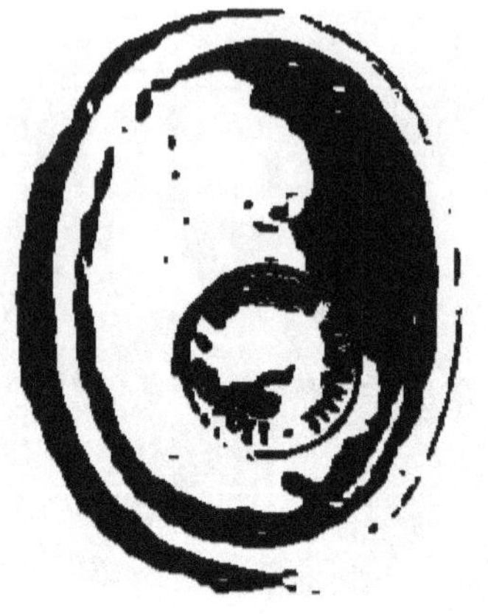

Sapho ou lee .Ld. Montague
[illegible]

Neptune on Gem [illegible] M.D.
[illegible]

Jupiter on Car.. J.ⁿ Wathergill M.D.

According to Act of Parliament. [illegible]

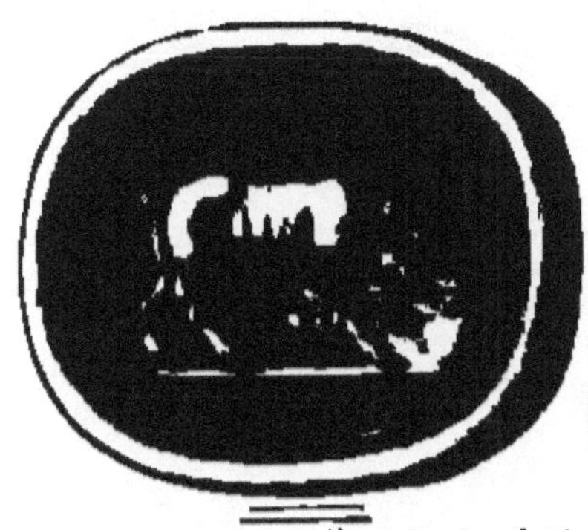

A Bull on a Ber. Ld Clanbrasill

[illegible] Parliament [illegible]

Medusa on Calcedon [illegible].

According to Act of Parliament [illegible]

Sabinus in Coll. Matthew Duane Esq.
According to Act of Parliament [illegible]

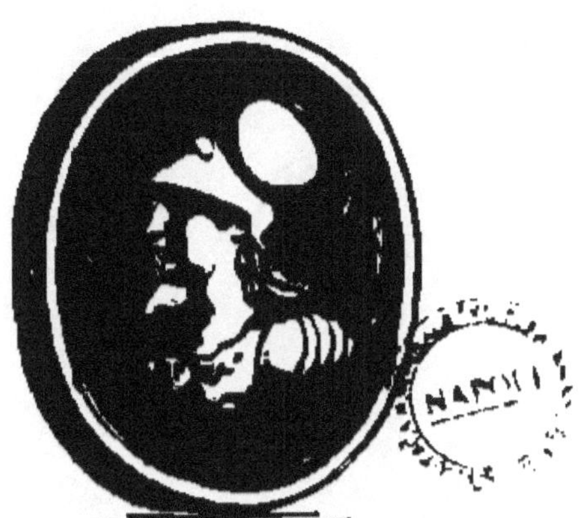

Minerva in Coll. Ld. Carlisle

According to the Act of Parliam.t [illegible] sc

Julius Caesar, on Calced[illegible] Montague

[illegible]

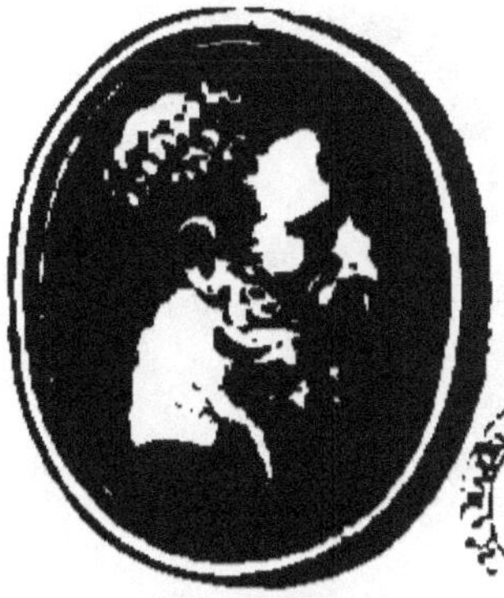

Hercules, on the Duke of Marlborough

[illegible]

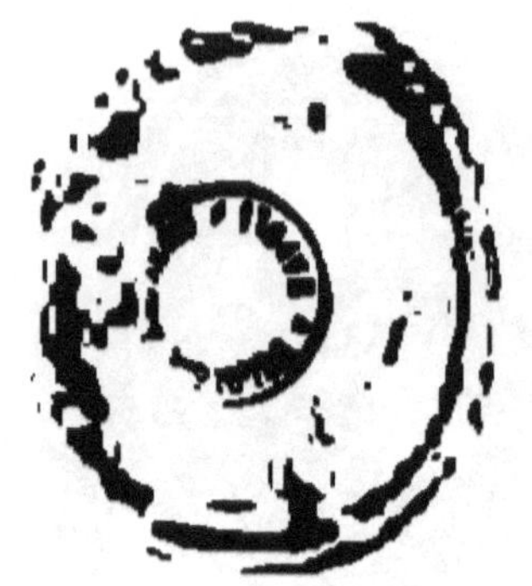

Semiramis, on the Duke of Marlborough

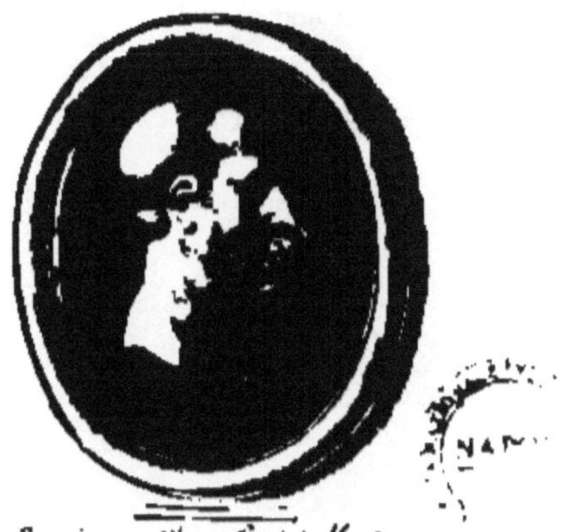

Scipio, on Cor. Lord C. Montague

Apollo [illegible]

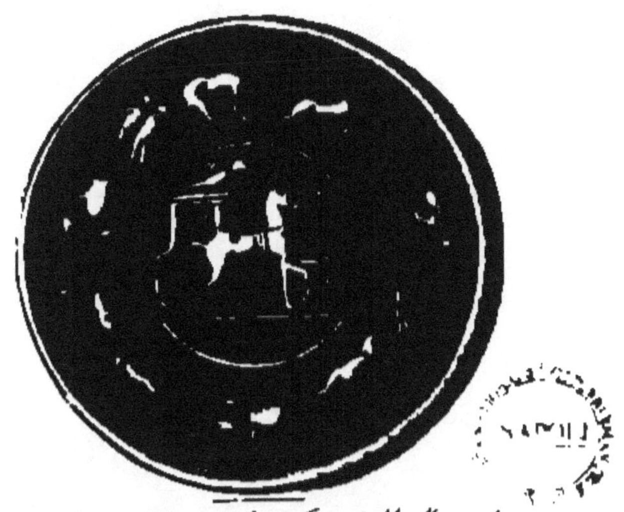

Zodiac & Quadriga on Sardon. D. of Marlborough.

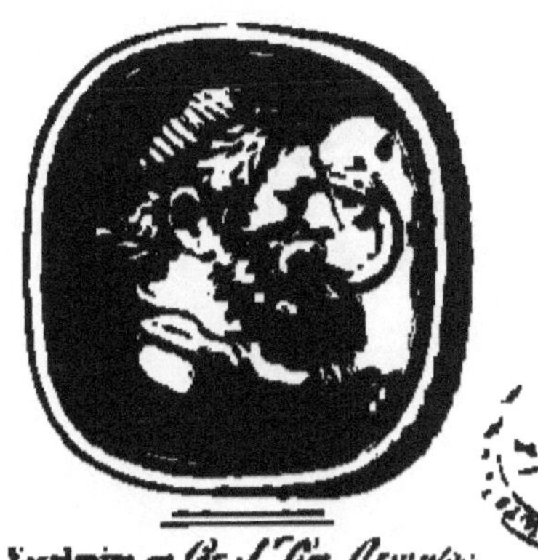

Aesculapius on Br. S.t Geo. Armytage's.

According to Act of Parliament [illegible]

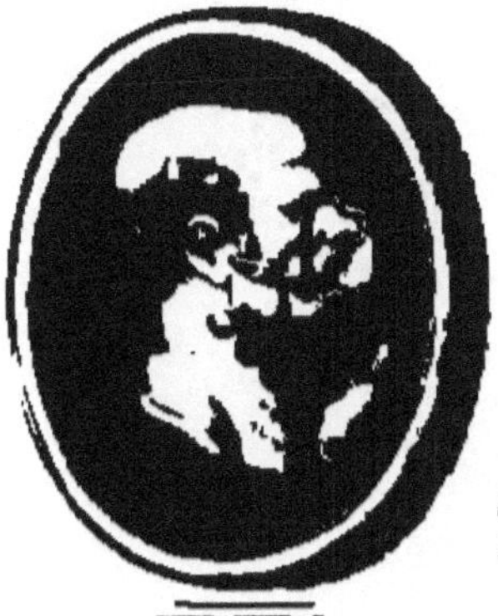

Socrates, on the Dutch's of Portland

[illegible]

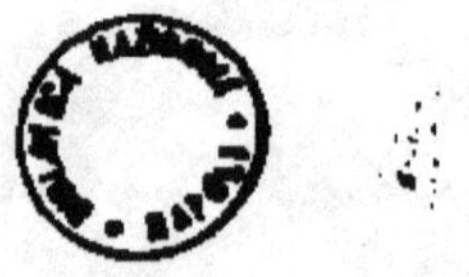

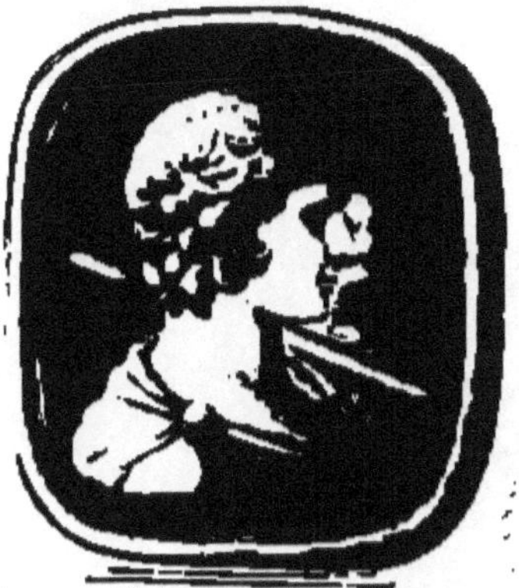

Antinous, on black. [illegible] of [illegible]

[illegible]

Sapho [illegible]

[illegible]

Mercury on Red Agate. Ld Montague

Cicero on Beryl · M. Hope

[illegible]

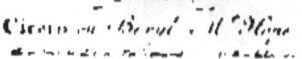

Infant Hercules on . Intaglio. Mat. Duane Esq.

[illegible]

Infant Hercules on [illegible]. Rich.d Duane Esq.r

[illegible] Act of Parliament [illegible]

Minerva on Cornelian Ld Montague.

According to Act of Parliament [illegible] sc.

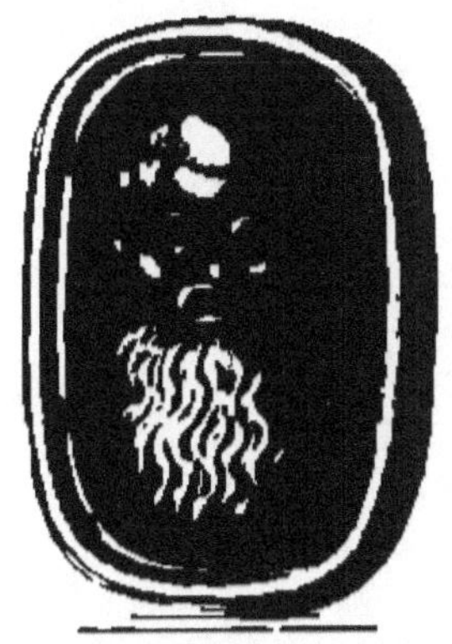

A [illegible] in the Duke of Marlborough

[illegible] sculp.

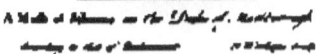

A Lyon [illegible]

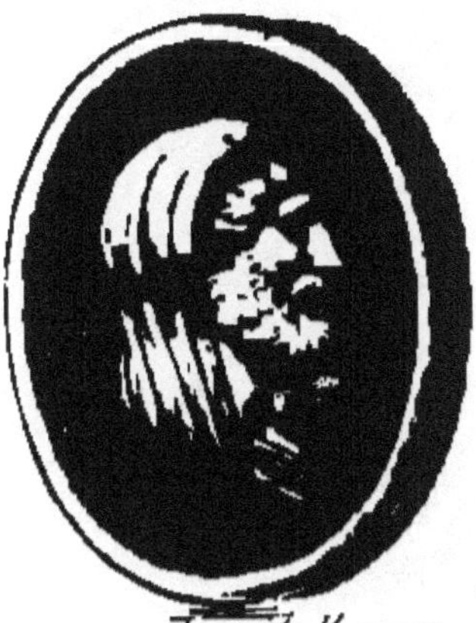

Neptune en Jasp. L.d. Montague

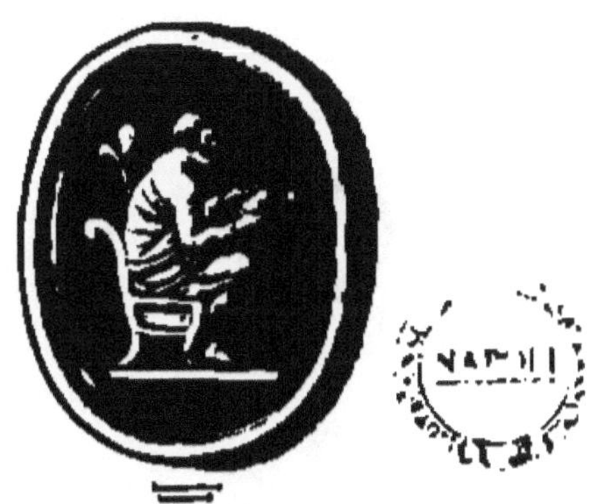

Philosopher, Owner ye Dutch.s of Portland

[illegible]

Medusa in Poss. Thos. Dundas Esq.

[illegible] of Parliament [illegible]

Cupid & Boar, on Cam. Thos. Dundas Esq.
according to Act of Parliament [illegible]

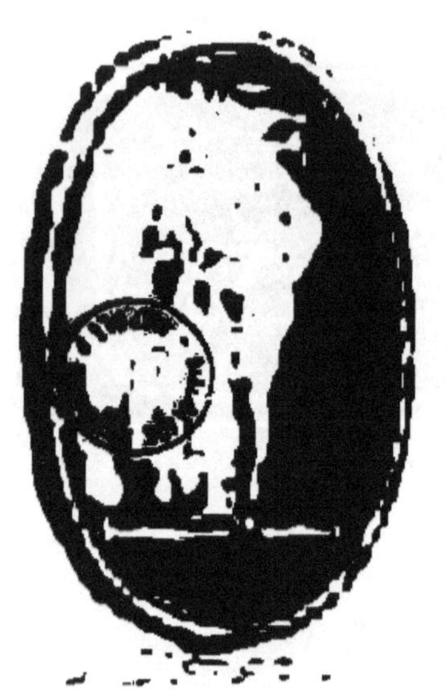

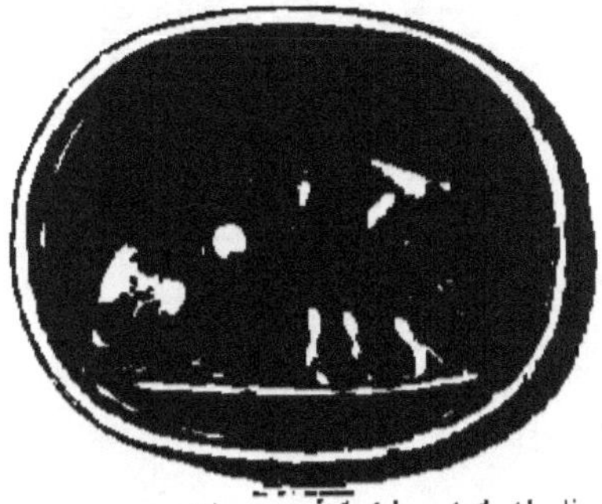

[illegible] Thos Dundas Esq
[illegible]

Dea della Salute en [illegible]

[illegible]

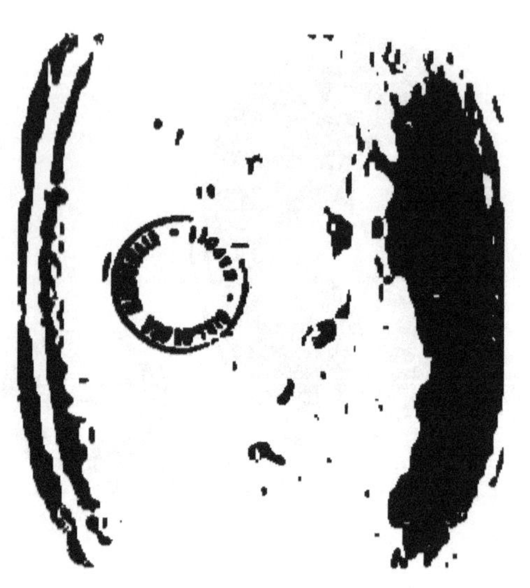

Apollo, on Cornelian, Duke of Marlborough ?

Published according to Act of Parliament

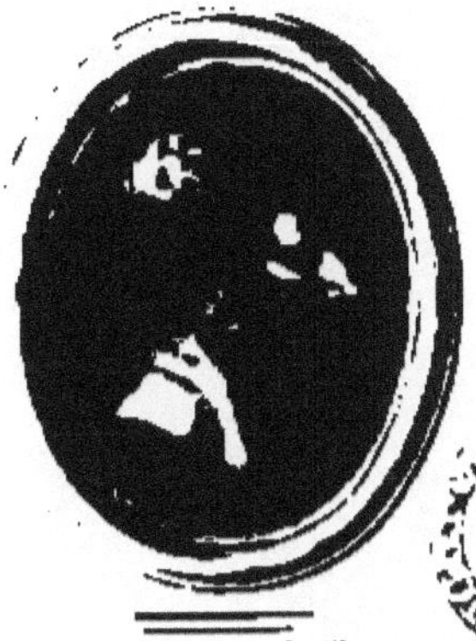

Caius Marius [illegible] Chauncey

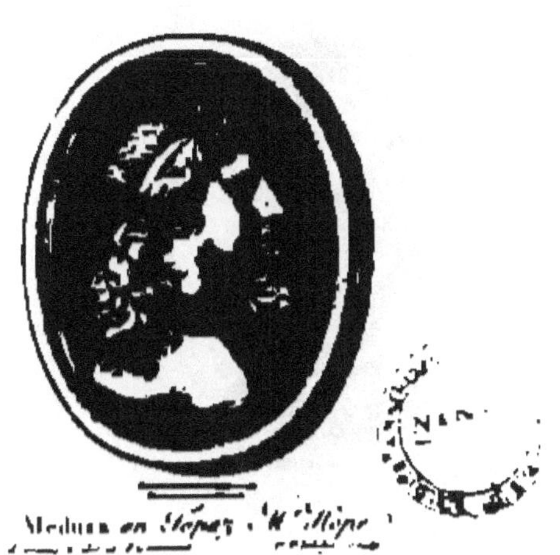

Medusa on Topaz (Mr Hope)

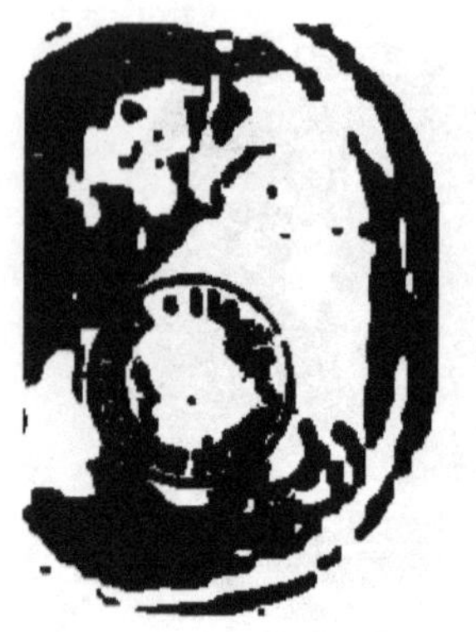

Cleopatra

Hercules bibax on the Duke of Marlborough

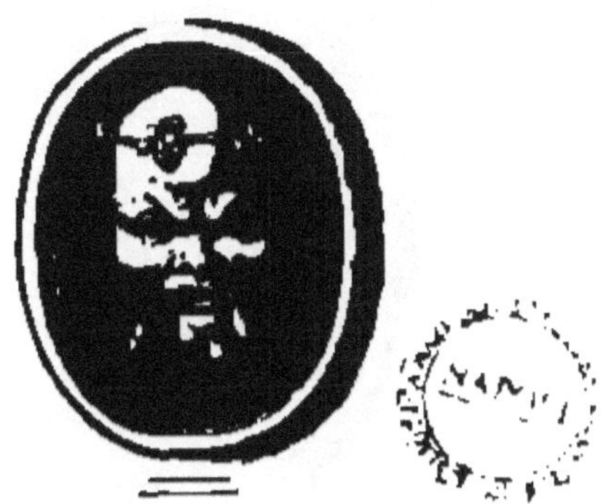

Silenus on Onyx Ld Clanbrassill.

[illegible]

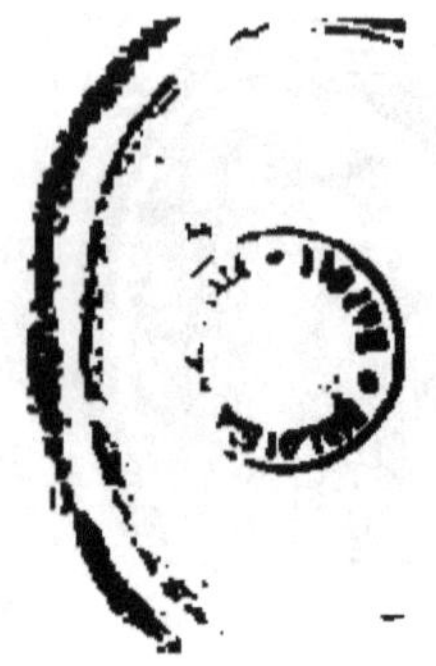

Diomede on White Agate. [illegible]

[illegible] Act of Parliament [illegible]

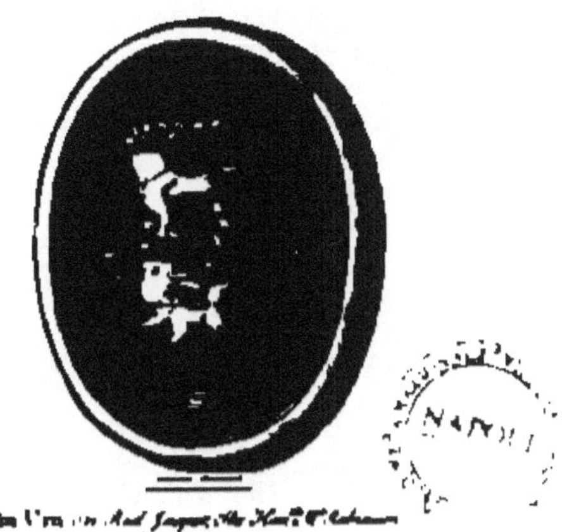

[illegible] Red Jasper, the [illegible]

[illegible]

Jupiter Serapis on Beryl. Mr Chauncey

According to Act of Parliament [illegible]

Horse &c. on Corn. Duke of Marlborough

According to Act of Parliament

A Bachanal on Gr. W. Stanley

Agrippina on Beryl Ld Besborough

Philip of Macedon on a Beryl [illegible]

according to Act of Parliament [illegible]

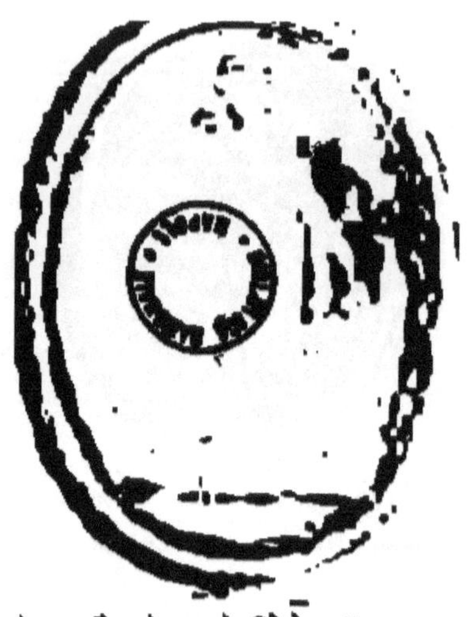

Mercury on Beryl Duke of Marlborough.

according to Act of Parliament [illegible]

Alexander in Cor. Ld. Besborough.

According to Act of Parliament. T. Worlidge sc.

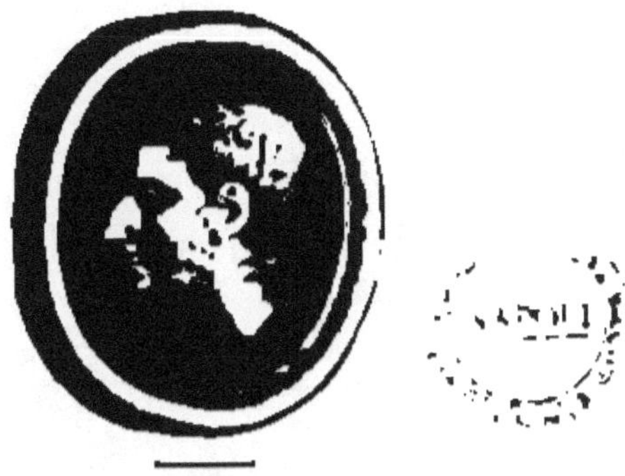

Tiberius [illegible]

[illegible]

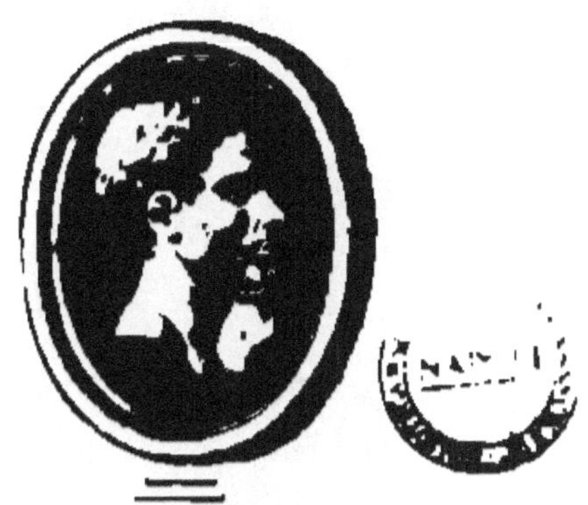

Marcus Brutus [illegible]

[illegible]

Ptolemy on a Topaz, L.d Besborough's

[illegible]

Jupiter Ammon [illegible]

[illegible]

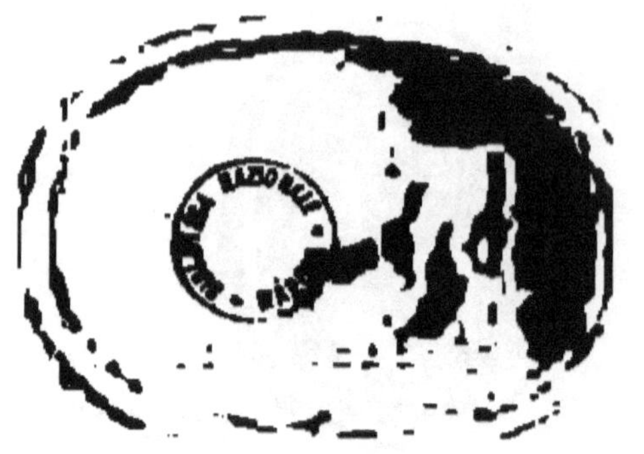

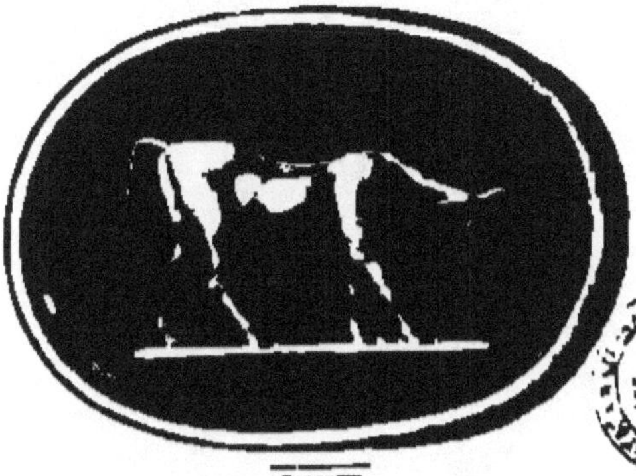

A Vacca, on Cow Dr Chauncey: —

[illegible]

Ptolemy on (Rev. Dr. Chauncy.

[illegible] Parliament, [illegible]

Lucilla on Beryl. Ld Besborough's

Carneolla [illegible]

[illegible]

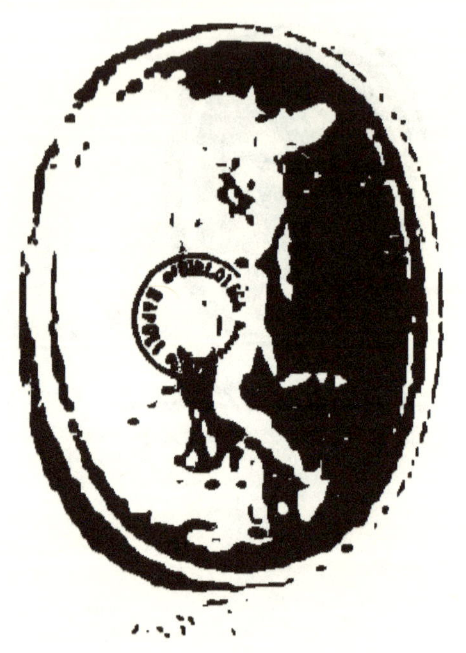

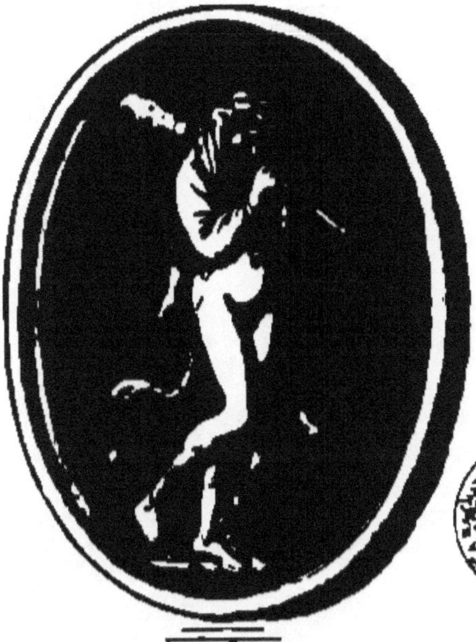

[illegible] Lᵈ Besborough.
[illegible]

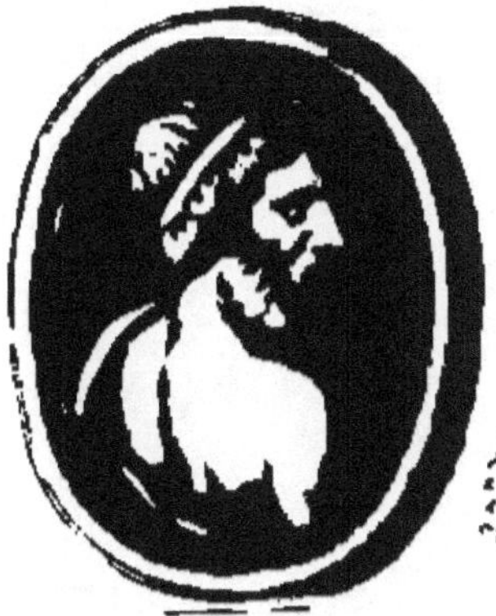

Pluto. in the Ld Bessborough.
[illegible]

Hannibal [illegible] late Ld Besborough [illegible]
[illegible]

Metrodorus ex Gem. Ld Besborough

According to Act of Parliament [illegible]

Sapho

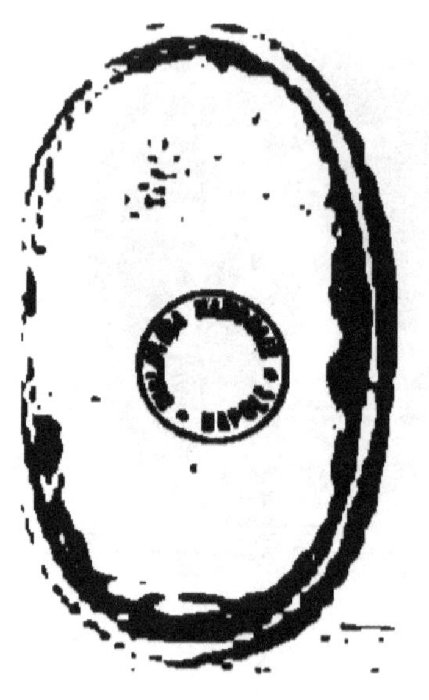

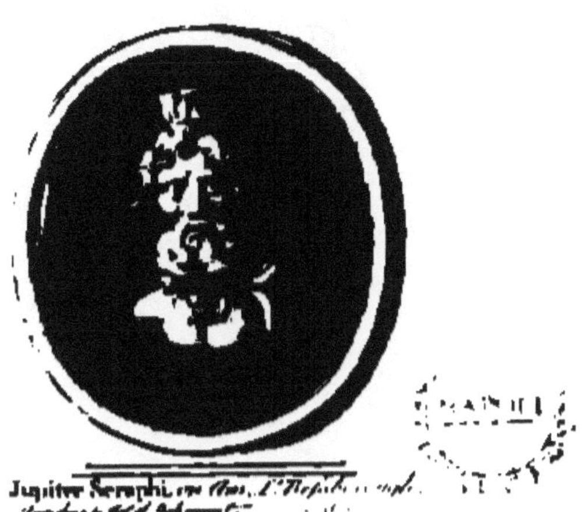

Jupiter Serapi[illegible]

A Faun [illegible]

Julia [illegible]

Scipio Africanus, [illegible]
[illegible]

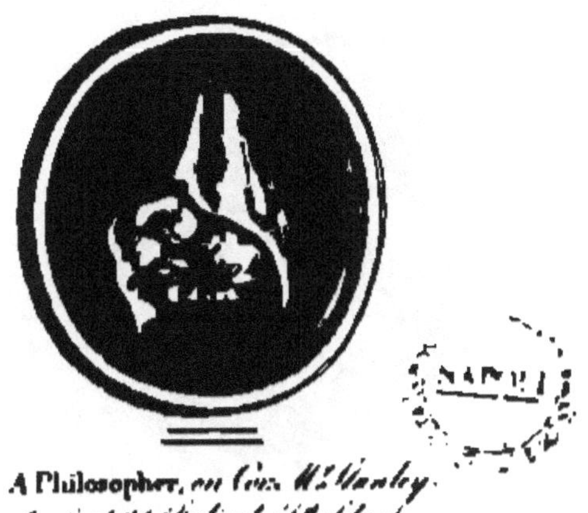

A Philosopher, on Corn. Mr. Manley.

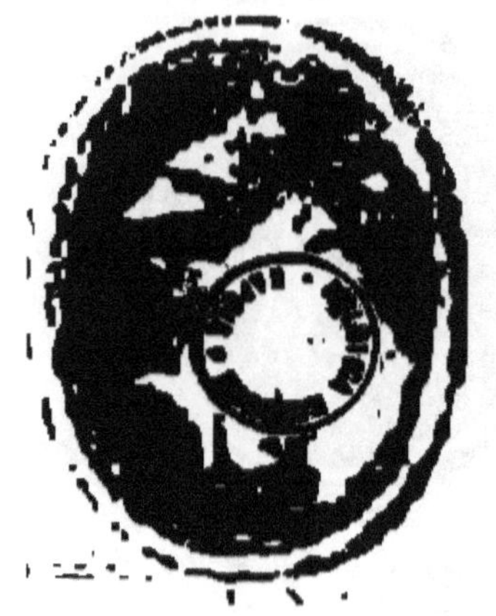

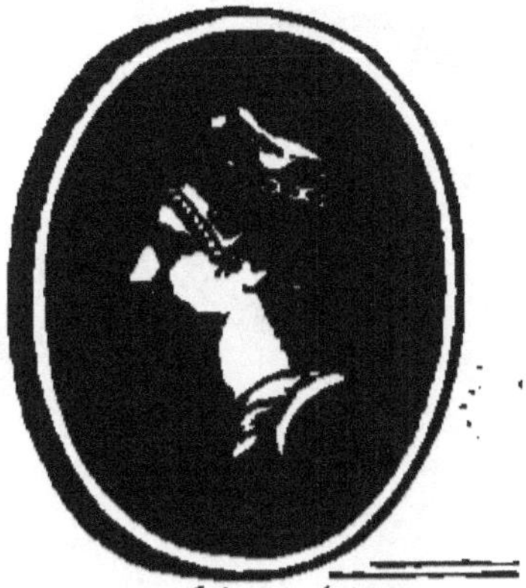

Sabina, on the Duke of Marlborough.

Bacchus on Beryl Ld Besborough. —

According to Act of Parliament [illegible]

Hercules, on Am. Cameo of Portland.

Epicurus, in Onyx D.r Chauncey.

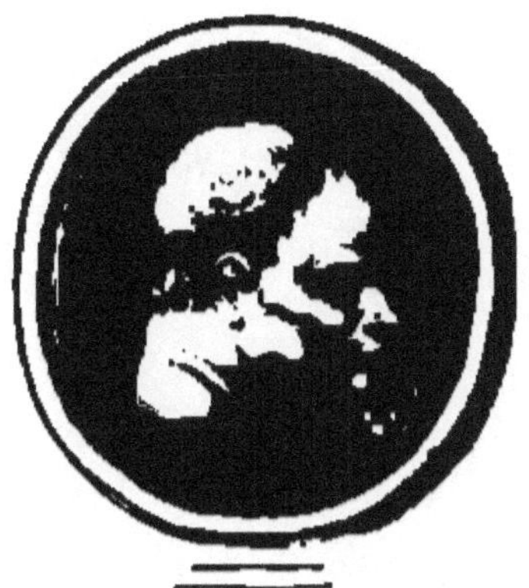

Vitellius, [illegible]
[illegible]

A Mask, on Beryl, M.r Hanley

[illegible]

Diomede & Ulysses on Sardo Duke of Marlborough.

[illegible]

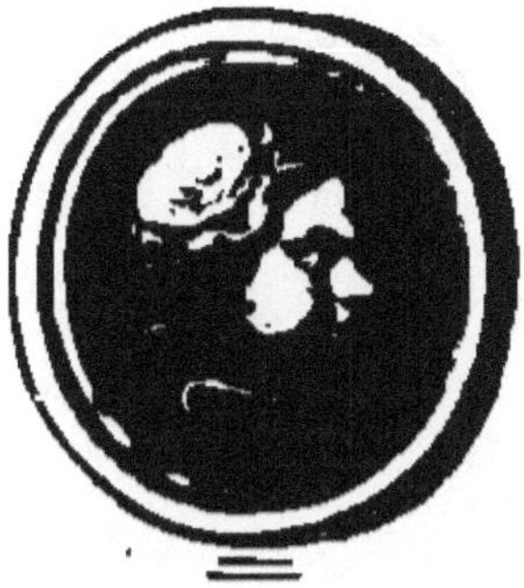

A Faun on Her. Lord Warwick

According to Act of Parliament [illegible]

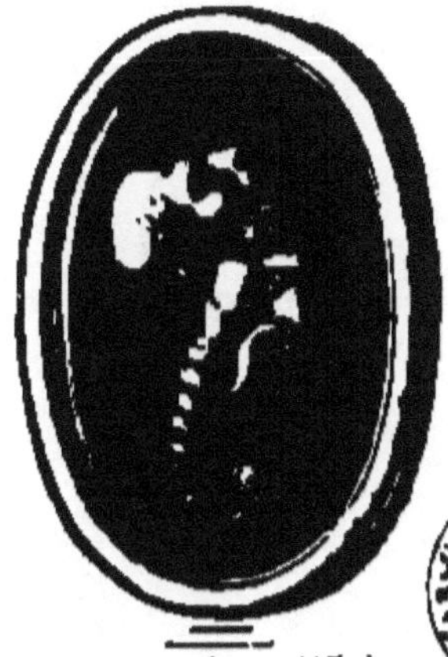

Chimera on Sar. Mr. Stanley

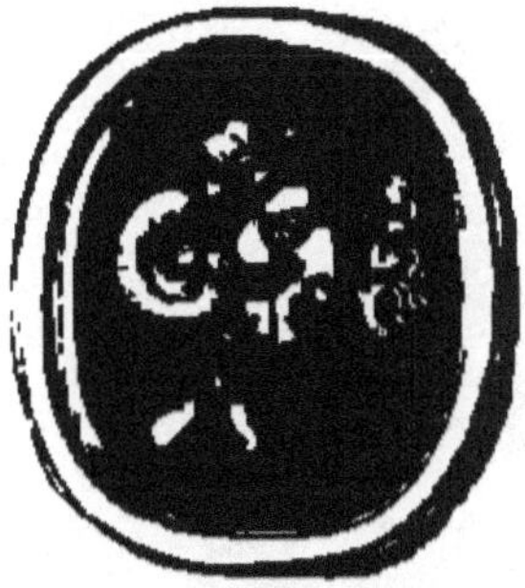

Jupiter Ammon on the

Duke of Leeds

[illegible]

Centaurs, on Am. Duke of Leeds.

Agrippa, on Beryl. Lord Grey

[illegible]

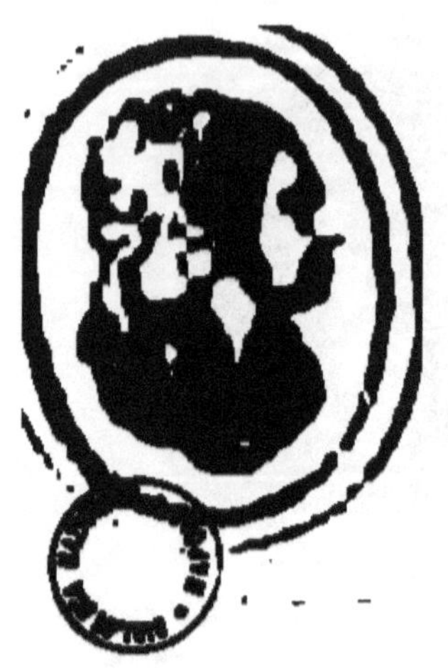

A Lion, on Cats Eye. Philip Carteret Webb Esq.

According to Act of Parliament

NAPOLI

Jupiter on Garnet. Duke of Portland

[illegible]

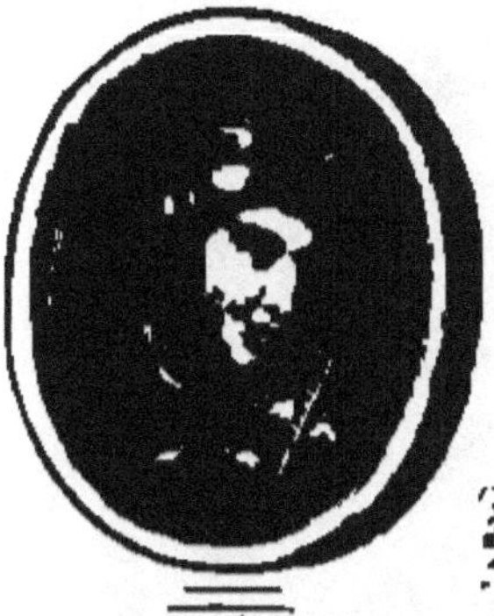

Mercury, on the Ld. Besborough
[illegible]

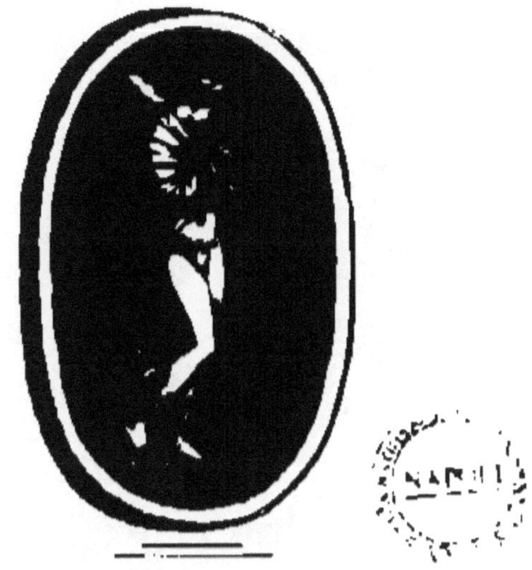

Iolo on . Amethyst Duke of Devonshire

According to Act of Parliament

Germanicus Caesar [illegible] W. Seymour
According to Act of Parliament [illegible]

Hercules [illegible] *Duke of* [illegible]

[illegible] Act of Parliament [illegible]

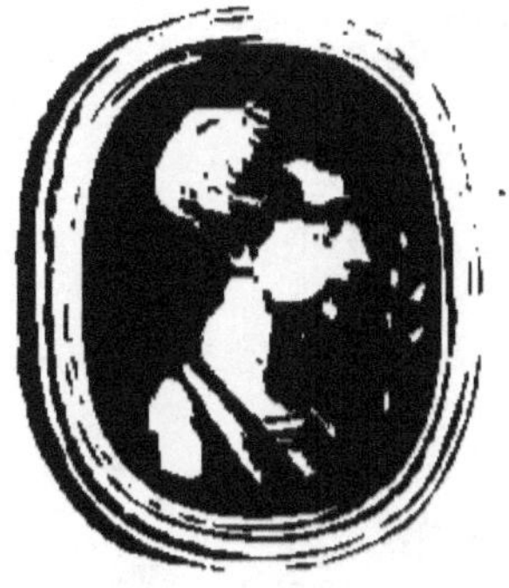

Horace, en Bec. Lord Gray

Antiochus on Onyx. W. Seymour

[illegible]

Pompey; on Aqua-Marine, [illegible]

According to Act of Parliament. [illegible]

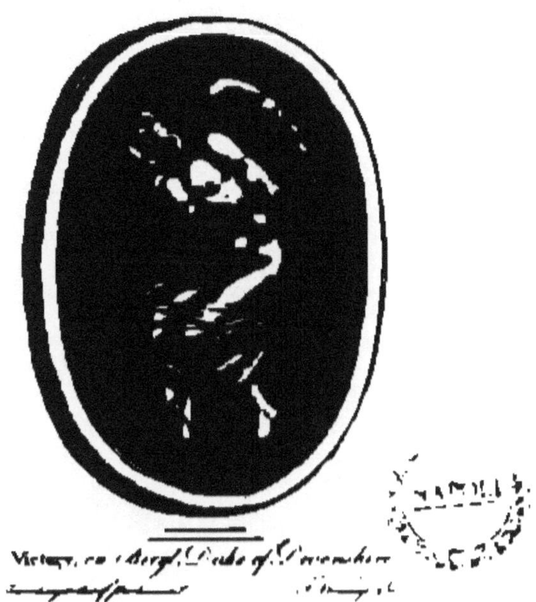

Victory, on a Beryl, Duke of Devonshire

A Girl, on Topaz, D. of Devonshire.

Augustus & Livia, on Corn. Mr. Stanley

[illegible]

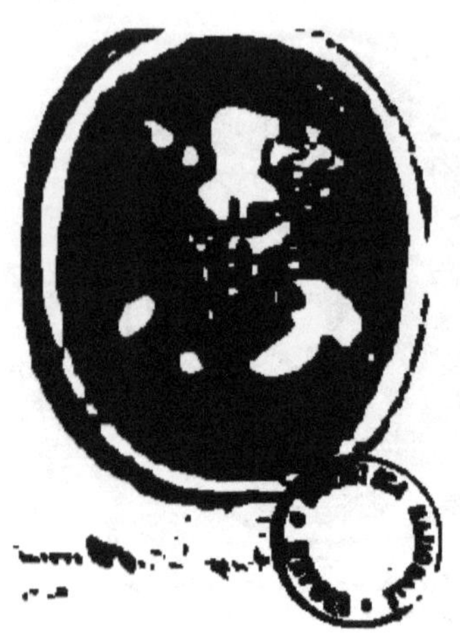

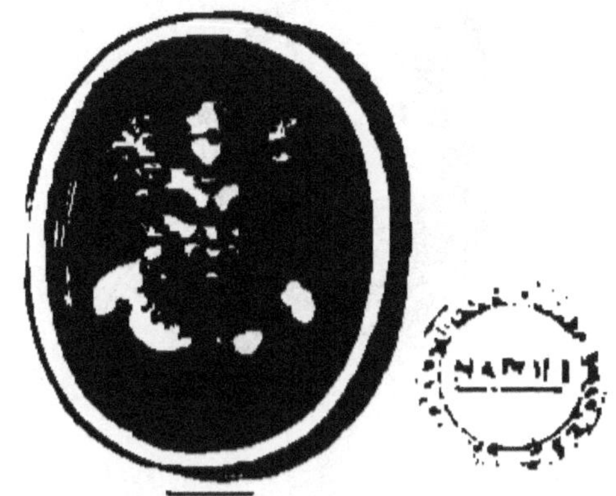

Silenus, on Sardonyx, D. of Devonshire.

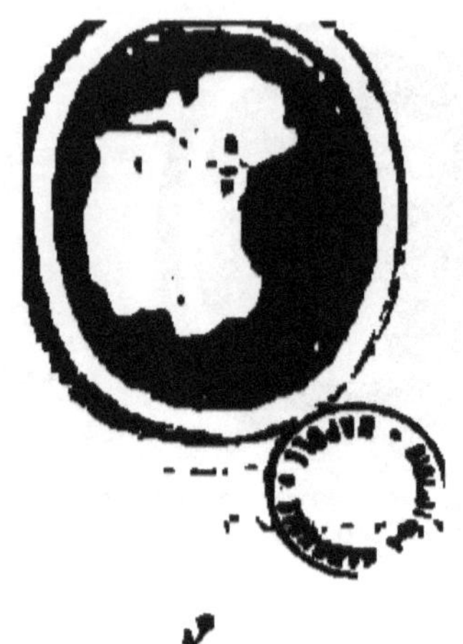

Poppæa on Calced. Earl of Essex. —

([illegible] of [illegible] [illegible])

Heliogabalus & Julia Paula,

In the Collectⁿ of the Earl of Radnor.

A Woman's Head [illegible] Duke of Devonshire

[illegible]

Hercules with a Bull on the [illegible]

[illegible]

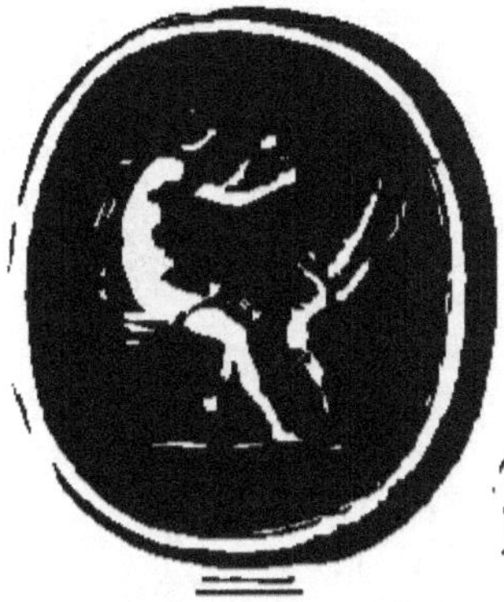

Jupiter & Leda, [illegible]

[illegible]

Salvator Mundi [illegible]
[illegible]

Tragic Muse,

Discobulus on Beryl, Ld Marlborough

According to Act of Parliament

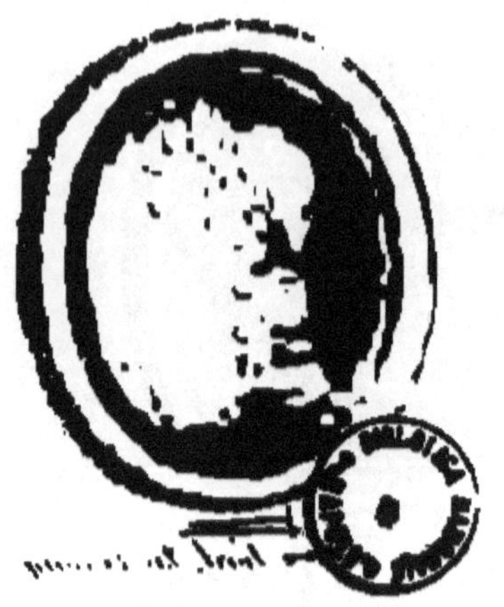

Apollo, on Cor. Lord Besborough.

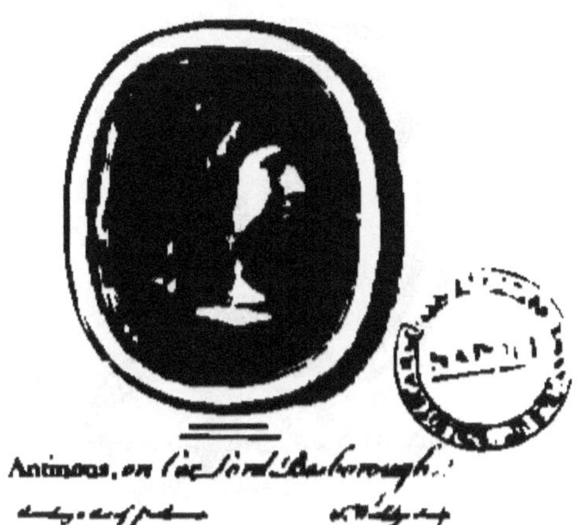

Antinous, on the Lord Besborough's

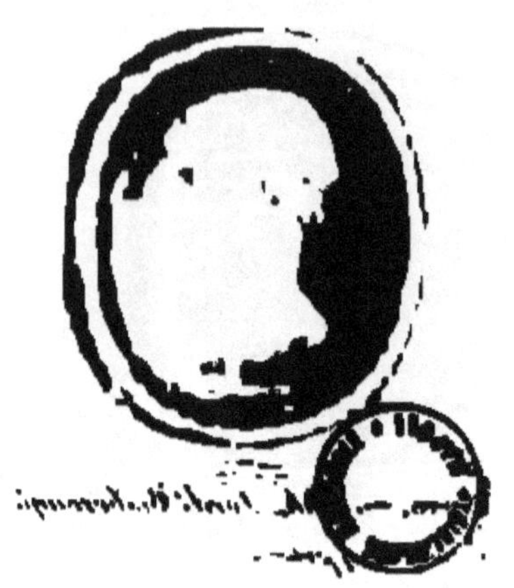

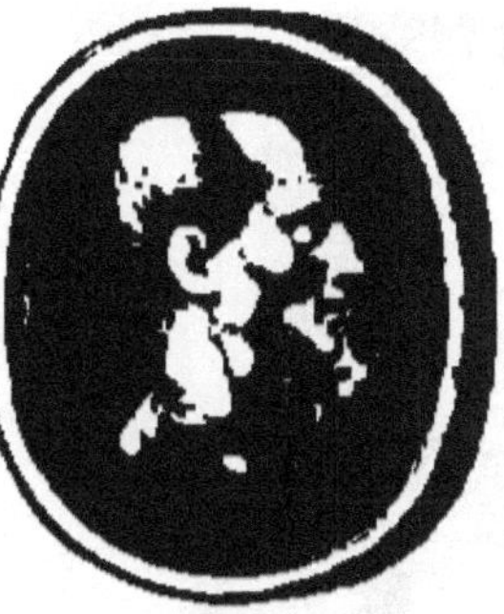

Cicero, on a Saph — Lord Besborough.

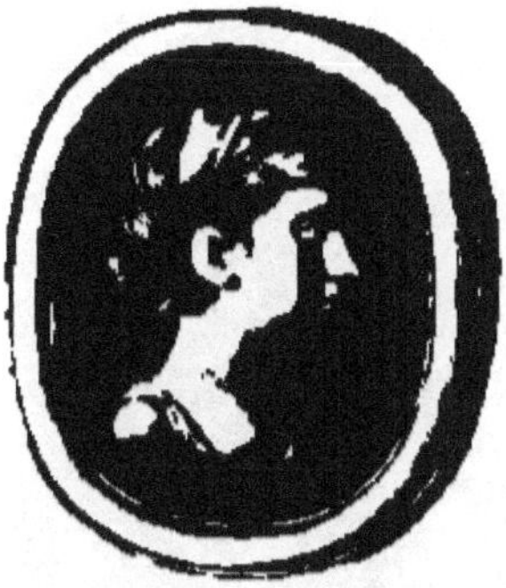

Sapho, on a Plasm, Lord. Besborough

Hercules Reposing, *on gr.n jasp. Duke of Devonshire*

Achilles. on Beryl. Duke of Devonshire

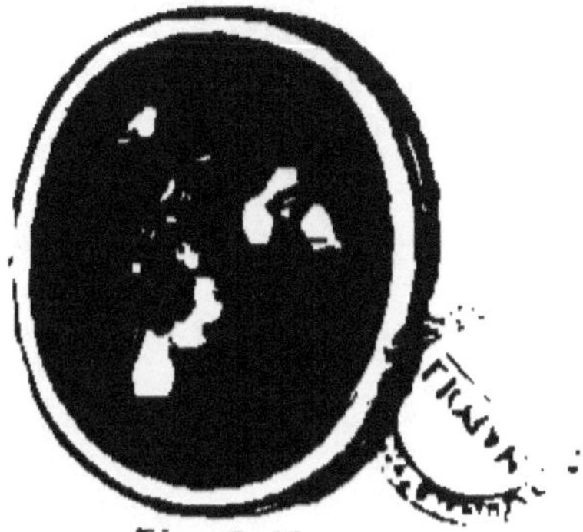

— on Cox D. of Devonshire

[illegible]

Ceres, on [illegible] Bishop of Llandaff.

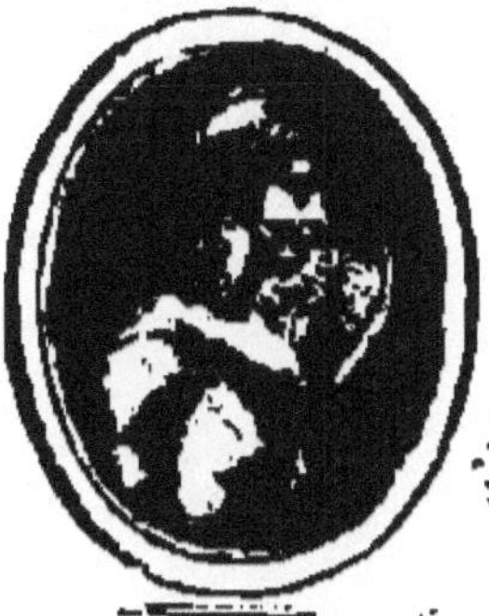

Apollo, en Ag. Baron Stosch,

A Bull Drinking on Cor: Duke of Devonshire.

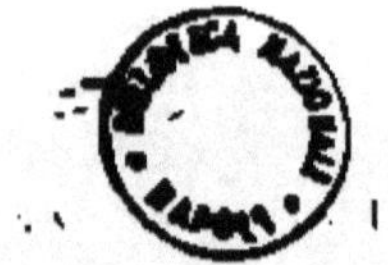

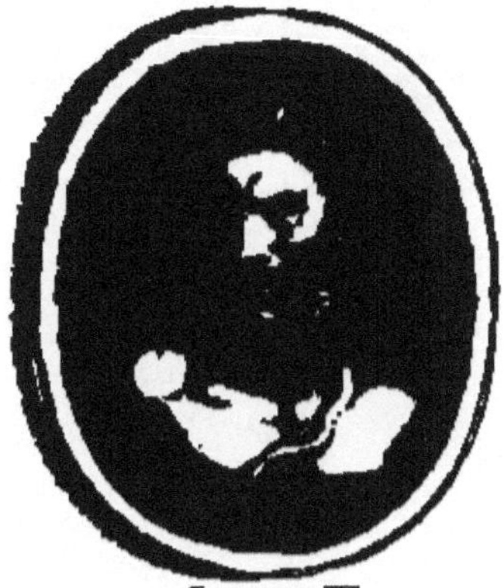

Laocum on Pastel W. Stanley.

Sabina on Agate. Mus. D. of Devonshire

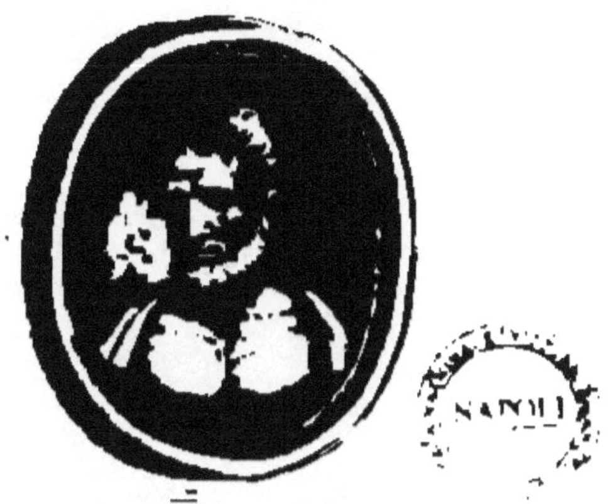

A Philosophier [illegible]

Selenus, on Cor. D. of Devonshire.

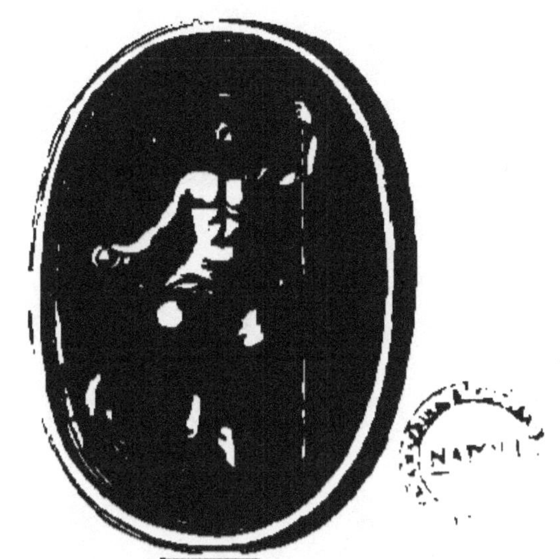

Jupiter Tonans, on Crystal L.d Montague

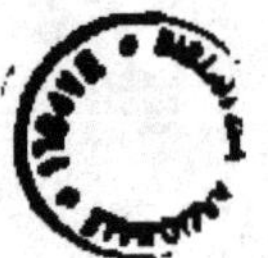

Alexander Severus

Domitian *[illegible] Lord Montagu*

Minerva on Onyx L.d Montague

A Sow on Plasma Ld Montague

Æsculapius on [illegible] Montagu [illegible]

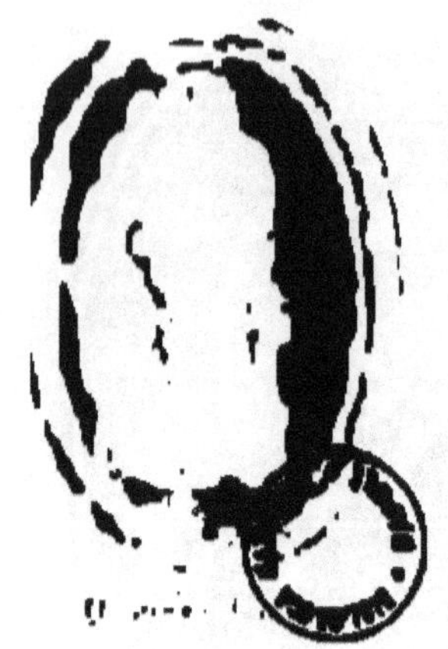

Female Figure, on Giacinto Quamacino

Lord Montagu.

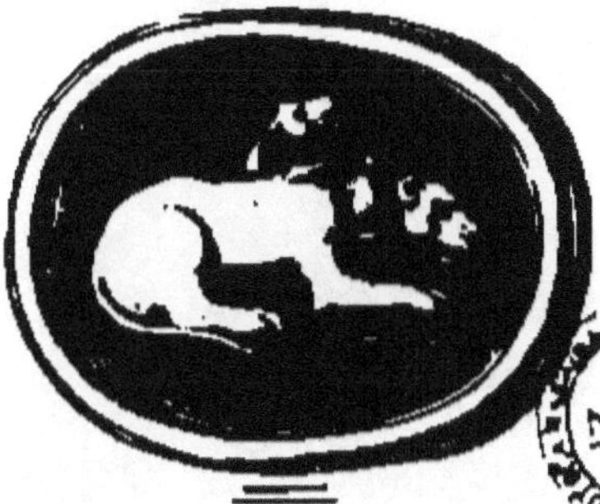

Chimera, on [illegible] Lord Montague.

[illegible] [illegible]

Bacchus, [illegible]

Tiger, on Onyx, Lord Montagu.

tion, on Yellow Cor. Lord. Montagu

Perseus, on Onyx. _ Lord Montague.

[illegible]

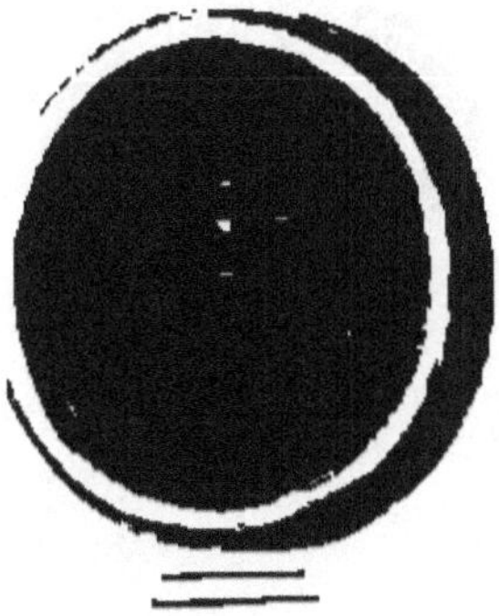

A Wasp, on Sicilian Jasp. B. Montague.

[illegible]

Hercules on Cup. Lord. Montague

A Cock on Red Jasper. L.d Montague

Cupid on *Lapis Laz. Lord Montague.*

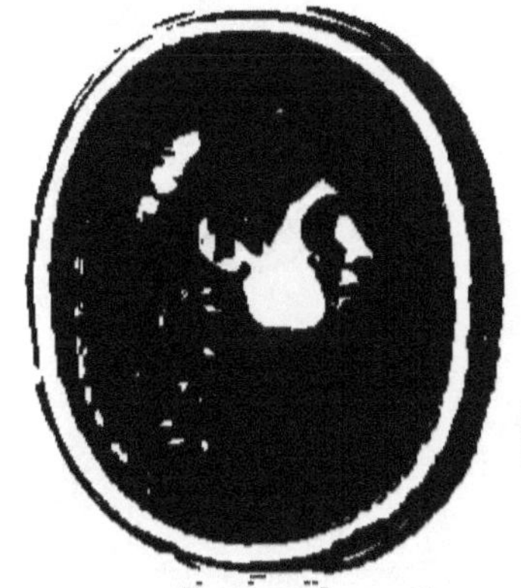

Apollo on Black Agate, Lord Cooke

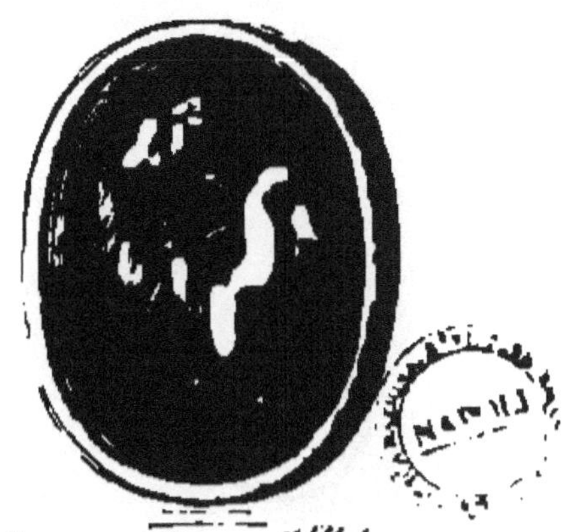

Originale [illegible] M. Walker.

[illegible]

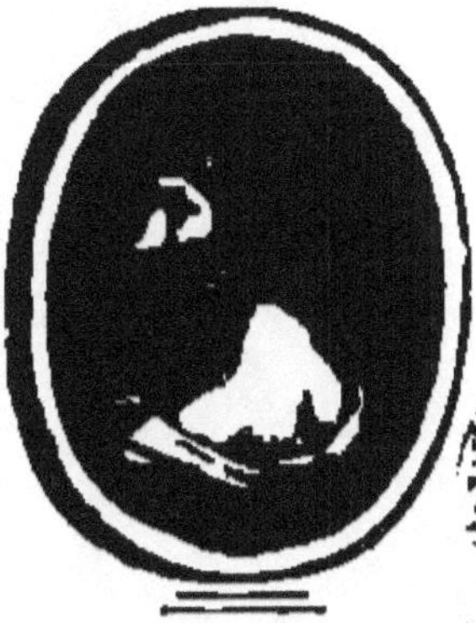

Ulysses ou [illegible])

[illegible]

Cyrus on Coins [illegible]

[illegible]

www.ingramcontent.com/pod-product-compliance
Lightning Source LLC
Chambersburg PA
CBHW030822110726
47900CB00006B/1702

* 9 7 8 3 7 4 2 8 1 9 3 0 7 *